ALL KNEELING

Books by
ANNE PARRISH

. . . .

A POCKETFUL OF POSES

SEMI-ATTACHED

LUSTRES (*with Dillwyn Parrish*)

THE PERENNIAL BACHELOR

TOMORROW MORNING

ALL KNEELING

. . . .

Harper & Brothers
Publishers

ALL KNEELING

BY

ANNE PARRISH (Mrs. Charles Albert Corliss) 18

HARPER & BROTHERS PUBLISHERS
NEW YORK AND LONDON
1928

ALL KNEELING

FOR
MARY POWERS

"To be said by the whole congregation . . . all kneeling."

— THE BOOK OF COMMON PRAYER

ALL KNEELING

ALL
KNEELING

Chapter One

CHRISTABEL CAINE sat by her open window writing "A Pleasant Incident of My Vacation" in the moments when there was nothing to distract her attention. But a good deal was happening that afternoon. Three times the door bell rang in quick succession, and she heard Katie Sullivan muttering: "Ring, ring, ring! God save us!" as she pounded to the door, heard the rattle and slam of bureau drawers from her mother's room.

Great-aunt Ann came first. The brougham glittered in the sun; Prince jingled his harness. Then the Shady Lawn victoria. Plum-colored Albert jumping down from the box, he and Aunt Clara helping out the small, slow, important bundle that was Great-aunt Deborah.

Last, the anticlimax of Mrs. Plummer, with her yearning stretch of chin and stringy neck, and the Bersagliere hat she wore "because of my Italy," propping her bicycle against the fence.

Hearing her mother's silk petticoat descend, Christabel took pad and pencil out to the piece-box at the top of the stairs in order not to miss anything, and presently heard her name.

"I wanted to ask you if you thought Christabel would be in a little play I've written for the children, a little fantasy, Princess Brighteyes and Prince Trueheart, I called it ——"

"Thee couldn't have made a better choice for Princess Brighteyes," Aunt Ann said, and Mrs. Plummer answered, nervously:

"Well, as a matter of fact—hm!—you see I felt that since Christabel was going to be the leading lady in the little French play—Mademoiselle Soulas happened to tell me—and Annette Perry says she's having her do the solo dance at the dancing-school exhibition, why, I thought it wasn't fair to Christabel to ask

2

her to do anything that would take too much time, so I—hm! hm! I asked little Helen Barnes to be Princess Brighteyes——"

"Asked who?" Aunt Deborah questioned.

"Asked Helen Barnes," Aunt Ann said, coldly. "Thee knows, Sister Deborah, that stout plain child, Caleb Barnes' grand-daughter."

"Thee means the child with the large front teeth?"

"Of course I would rather have had Christabel, but since I *asked* little Helen Barnes——"

"Oh yes, of *course*. And Christabel *is* very busy," Mrs. Caine murmured, politely.

"A court lady seems a very tiny part to offer Christabel, such a born little actress."

Helen Barnes! Christabel thought. I just despise that old Helen Barnes! I wouldn't be in that old play for anything——

But a vision of herself as a court lady floated before her. Only a court lady, but simply taking the shine out of Princess Brighteyes. She

3

could see herself, in her mother's new claret-colored evening dress, unconscious, lost in her part; she could hear people saying: "Who is that exquisite child with the sensitive face? See, she has forgotten it isn't real; she *is* a court lady. The other children are acting their parts, but she is living hers." "Yes, mother dear," she whispered. "Yes, Mrs. Plummer, I'll *try* to be a court lady ———"

The conversation moved on from her and was no longer interesting. But still she hung over the banisters, for she had caught sight of her reflection in the glass of an engraving of the Sistine Madonna, and gazed at herself against a background of saints and angels until her mother's voice broke the enchantment and sent her tiptoeing back to her room before she answered, "Yes, mother dear?"

"Come down a minute, darling."

In the mirror over the fireplace Christabel saw herself again as she laid her smooth peach-pink cheek against the great-aunts' withered dead-leaf faces, Aunt Clara's doughy whiteness, Mrs. Plummer's sallowness. Dark bright eyes with fringing lashes, dark auburn satin hair, feathers of eyebrows delicately drawn on a white brow. She went back and gave Aunt Ann, who was sitting opposite the mirror, an extra hug.

"Mrs. Plummer wants to know if you will take part in a little play she's written, darling."

"Princess Brighteyes and Prince Trueheart —I want you to be one of the court ladies, dear. I'm afraid it's a very tiny part, but ——"

"Oh, *thank* you, Mrs. Plummer. I'd *love* to. I'll *try* to be a court lady."

Aunt Ann and Aunt Deborah exchanged proud glances, and Aunt Clara whispered a piercing "Sweet!" As for Amy Caine, she threw her arms about her little daughter and kissed her.

"No, Christabel, you can*not* wear my red silk. Now, come, be mother's dear little daughter and get into your costume."

5

Sobs from the floor where Christabel had cast herself.

"Come, Christabel."

Heartbroken moans.

"You look so *sweet* in your costume; everyone said so when you wore it at Ernestine's party."

On the bed lay the chintz panniers and net fichu that might have represented Martha Washington or The Sweetest Girl in Dixie or just that faithful stand-by, Old-fashioned Lady. With her face still hidden, Christabel kicked in its direction and cried in a muffled voice:

"I'd rather *die!*"

"Now, Christabel, get up and wash your face. Mother's simply astonished! A big girl like you! Nobody's going to notice your costume. Come ——"

"No! No! *No-o-o!*"

The front door slammed. Mr. Caine had come home early to accompany his ladies to

6

the house that all Germantown spoke of as the Edith Johnson Plummers'.

"Christabel, there's father! You don't want him to see you acting like a baby."

"Oh, *fah*-h-h-ther!"

"Hell*o*! What's the matter with my little girl?"

"The child's got a notion in her head that nothing will do but to wear my new red silk— and here's her own nice costume ———"

"Oh, father, I'd rather die than wear that horrible old thing. You'd be so *ashamed* of me!"

"Amy ———"

He nodded meaningly toward the hall, and Mrs. Caine followed him out, closing the door. Christabel's sobs stopped; she lay rigid, listening to the murmur of voices. Then, stepping out of her slippers, she tiptoed to the door and pressed against it.

"Well, but, Fred—all those children! And Edith Plummer'll probably have something messy like ice-cream afterward, and it'll be my

7

only new dress this winter. Do you really think——?"

"Did you notice what was worrying her? She wasn't thinking of herself; she was afraid *we'd* be ashamed of her."

Tears flooded Christabel's eyes again; her lip quivered. I *only* want them to be proud of me, she thought. That's the only reason I'm being in this awful old play, just to *try* to make them happy.

"I know, bless her heart! She's thrown herself into this as if the whole thing depended on her. You know that's the only reason I *would* like to let her wear what she wants, she's been so sweet about having such a tiny little part; never a word of complaint, and you know it *would* have been natural. I don't know when she hasn't had the leading part in really everything. Of course it's none of my business, but I can't help feeling it's a *lit*tle funny of Edith Plummer——"

"I'd let her wear it."

"Well—I will, then."

8

Christabel left the door and stepped into her slippers. Just below her chest was a spreading warmth, a tingling that flowed through her. *Darling* mother and father, she thought, and suddenly lifted her shoulder and quickly, lightly kissed it.

When she saw herself in the mirror, hair turned up from smooth white neck, eyelashes stuck into points by forgotten tears, exquisite in the claret-colored silk with its pouring train, she flung her arms tight around her mother's neck and cried: "Oh, mother dear, you're so *good* to me! I'm so happy I think I'll die!" But in the Edith Johnson Plummers' library she was no longer happy. No one was noticing the court lady, except her father and mother. Helen Barnes, in Mrs. Barnes' white satin dress and a gilt paper crown, was getting all the attention.

"Sweet Princess Brighteyes," Prince Trueheart said, belligerently, and paused.

"From afar ——" Mrs. Plummer prompted.

"From afar."

9

"I come ——"

"Oh yes—from afar *I* come

To beg thee, lovelia *swun*, to share *my* throne."

And the insufferable Princess Brighteyes replied:

"Nay, thooth, Printh Trueheart, that may *neve*r be."

Silence from the Prince.

"Pray, dost thou love ——" from Mrs. Plummer.

"Oh yes—Pray does thou love another more *than* me?"

"Nay, but on me there reththth a cruel thpell. Draw clother, and the thtory I will tell."

"Heavens!"

"Get out of the way, children!"

"What's happened?"

"One of the children's fainted—Christabel Caine."

"Here—put her here on the sofa ——"

"Look *out*, children!"

10

"Here's the water!" cried some one, sprinkling it all over the claret-colored silk.

"Poor little thing, the excitement was too much for her!"

"So highly strung ——"

"Isn't it unusual for a person who's fainted to have such high color?" Helen Barnes' mother asked. "The child's cheeks are scarlet."

Christabel stirred, moaned faintly.

"She's coming to!"

Christabel opened her eyes and saw people kneeling about her, saw the scared and solemn children on the outskirts. Princess Brighteyes' crown had been knocked off in the excitement. "Where am I?" the court lady murmured, and then, "*Mother* ——!" and buried her face in Mrs. Caine's bosom.

"There, darling, *there!* Now you're all right. Now my Christabel's all right!"

"Well, well! What a girl, to give us such a fright!"

"Father!" She put out a weeping-willow hand.

"Hadn't we better take her home?"

"Oh, no, *no!* I don't want to spoil the play. I'm—all right." She smiled bravely.

"Are you *sure* you're all right, darling?"

"Oh yes, mother dear, but, *oh*, did I spoil the play?"

"Did you hear that?"

"Ah-h-h! Sweet!"

"I really don't think it would hurt her to stay, Fred."

"Look, she can sit right here in this big arm-chair, just like a throne!"

"Yes, just like a throne for little Queen Christabel!"

"Mother?"

"Right here, darling, and father's on the other side. And any time you'd rather go, just tell us."

"Mother, will Mrs. Plummer forgive me for spoiling the play?"

"Mrs. Plummer, we want to know if you'll forgive us?"

"Well, I just guess Mrs. Plummer *will!*

12

And now," said Mrs. Plummer, with a playful curtsy, "is it Your Majesty's wish that the play go on? All right, children. Shoo, shoo, shoo! Let's get back to our places. Let's see, Helen, where had you gotten to? Does anyone remember?"

The children fumbled for their lines. The command performance proceeded.

Chapter Two

ON THE whole, Christabel approved of her
family and her surroundings. The
house in which she grew up was small and
rather shabby, but carriages with coachmen and
footmen stopped at it, bringing hothouse grapes
to lie in the fruit-dish on the sideboard, hothouse flowers to fill the vases. And lack of
money could be bravely borne, since Aunt Ann
and Aunt Deborah sent her to boarding-school,
Aunt Lydia helped with her clothes, Aunt Susannah paid for the summer when she and five
other high-born maidens of Germantown followed Mrs. Plummer's yearning profile, flat
heels, and streaming cock-feathers through Ann
Hathaway's garden, the Louvre, and Saint
Peter's.

The great-aunts lived on estates with smooth
lawns, weeping trees, and formal flower-beds,
with names like Shady Lawn and The Cedars
—places that looked and sounded like high-

class cemeteries, Great-uncle Johnnie said.
Surrounded by old family servants, silver, por-
traits, by tribes of unmarried daughters and
widowed daughters-in-law, they made a rich
dim background against which Christabel felt
herself shining, simple and unspoiled.

The great-uncles were dead long ago, except
Uncle Johnnie, who had never married. He
had been engaged when he was young to a distant cousin, Ellen Caine, who had jilted him
and run away with her brother's tutor. That
had hardened him, Christabel feared. Because
really Uncle Johnnie was trying, sometimes.
He can't be happy, she decided, because real
happiness comes only with unselfishness, living
for others, and if anyone ever lived for himself, it was Uncle Johnnie. But he had the
appearance of enjoying life. He had a notable
wine cellar; he had a small glasshouse in
which he grew melons at the cost of about
forty-five dollars a melon; he had his boots
made to order; and he was fond of experiments
with port and cheese and time that made his

sisters fold their handkerchiefs about their
noses. And he had a disquieting way of looking as if some secret joke amused him. Christabel agreed with Aunt Clara, who said it was
such a pity for himself that Uncle Johnnie
seemed to like to laugh at people instead of with
them.

Among the great-aunts and the one great-
uncle Christabel felt like a flower in a November garden. But that was the sort of thing one
couldn't say about oneself. There were draw-
backs to being the only member of the family
that poetic description applied to, and the only
one who had a poetic imagination.

The great-aunts cherished their treasure, and
she loved them in return, finding their absurd-
ity touching, listening to the battles that raged
as to whose gardener could grow the best glox-
inias, to the battle-cry, "There, Sister Susannah, beat that if thee can!" and melting with
an ageless understanding. For they are such
children, she thought, only wanting to have the
biggest, never really seeing the velvety dark

blue petal curving against the light. But they, too, considered her a child, and sometimes she felt smothered by their solicitude. One day I will get away from it all and live my own life, she promised herself. No matter how hard it is, no matter how much I suffer, I must live. And she had bright pictures of herself living—somewhere, anywhere but in Germantown. She saw firelit faces turned toward her, young painters and writers gathered around her under the snow on a sloping roof. It was more vivid to her than the ballrooms where she danced with Caleb Barnes, 3d, or ate chicken salad with William James Russell, young gentlemen approved of by the aunts, who were, she feared, a tiny bit snobbish. If you only knew how little all this means to me, she would think with secret amusement, accepting a glass of lemonade from Caleb, smiling at William James.

For although she "came out" at a tea at Shady Lawn, carrying first Aunt Deborah's rosebuds frilled with lace, then Aunt Ann's

froglike orchids, before she permitted herself
Gerald Smith's red roses, although she went to
the Assemblies with Uncle Johnnie, and to all
the débutante parties, she was not just a society
butterfly. She wrote poems, and they were
sometimes printed in magazines.

It was through Aunt Susannah that she met
Talbot Emery Towne, the president of a small
refined publishing company. The three dined
together at The Cedars. Christabel, turning
her face from Aunt Susannah's withered cheeks
and watered silk to Mr. Towne's stock and silvery sideburns, felt herself dewy with youth,
tender with compassion toward age. Oh, poor
old darlings, she thought, gazing at them from
wide eyes whose starriness she felt herself, and
hearing vaguely something about literary London. Holding your little shields of memories,
pretty speeches, pheasant with bread sauce,
tawny port, between you and the Dark Archer
who draws near you. Her heart swelled with
pity as she answered, sweetly, "Yes, Aunt Susannah," or, "Oh, Mr. Towne, *really*?"

After dinner she followed Aunt Susannah's instructions and melted into the conservatory. She knew her poems were being shown to the publisher. She stood still, staring at a plant with big heart-shaped leaves, bronze-green, centered and splotched with pink. Her heart thudded as if it would shake her to pieces. But when in answer to, "Christabel, child, where is thee?" she went back to the drawing-room and saw Susannah's beaming face and the bland benevolence of Talbot Emery Towne's, each with a pot of green and pink-splotched leaves floating in the air above it, she knew her poems were as good as published.

The book appeared on a small select spring list: *A Pilgrim in Palestine*, by Lady Elizabeth Cook-Paynter; *I Remember, I Remember*, by Canon J. D. R. Wormsley; *Ask Me No More*, A Novel, by Caroline Trimmingham Wales; *The Pot Beneath the Thorn Bush*, by Eimar O'Sullivan, *Stars and Wild Strawberries*, by Christabel Caine——

Christabel Caine, Christabel Caine, *Stars*

and Wild Strawberries, by Christabel Caine. She came back to her name in print, over and over again. Christabel Caine ——

The day the book was published she sat at her desk, surrounded by propped-open copies whose drying ink said "For Aunt Deborah, with her Christabel's love," "Dearest love to Aunt Ann from Christabel," or, full of meaning, "Christabel to Gerald." Now and then she had to dip into a poem—"Cherry Blossoms," "The Old Pain," "Scarlet Slippers"— reading through her own eyes, through Gerald's, through the eyes of the new man at the dinner last night. Then through her own eyes again.

So young, so touched by the fire. I am dedicated to my work, I have chosen the difficult path, she thought. I have chosen the lonely way. And really Eleanor Atkinson's luncheon, the Palmers' box party at the Mask and Wig, even the walk up the Wissahickon she was going to take with Gerald if it ever stopped

20

raining, were unimportant to her compared with her book.

From her desk drawer she took an old composition book labeled "My Secret Journal," and wrote:

"It's been a wingéd day, because today

THE BOOK

has come. What can I say of this thing, a book of poems to others, but my Heart's Blood to me? My pain has gone to make it, and my petal dreams, and no one will know that I cut my feet on the stars when I gathered some of my Singing Words."

She read this, chewing the end of her pen, and added:

"God, give me a Brave Heart and a Singing Soul—give me courage to follow the Path Difficult."

All right for other girls to care about dresses and men and good times. They were not the dedicated spirits, the children of light. She had explained all this to Gerald; she would explain again. It isn't that I don't *like* fun, Gerald; it isn't that I don't long to play; but my work must come first. The last time they had had a good talk about her vocation Gerald had said, suddenly, "You have an awfully spiritual expression!"

She went to the mirror now to see if she had. And as she gazed the pure colors and clear outlines blurred, she slipped to her knees, and with uplifted face whispered, "I accept!"

"I can't understand her poems," Uncle Johnnie said to the aunts, flapping the pages this way and that. "What does this part mean, about building a house from the small bleached bones of a little field mouse? What does she mean by tired little tunes?"

"I think they're all lovely, and thee isn't required to understand poetry, Johnnie," Aunt Eliza answered. "Will thee have a cup of tea?"

22

"A glass of sherry and a biscuit, please. Now look here, Eliza, what's all this about?

> "My room is sweet and blue
>   (Cold is the white moon's breast),
> I will not think of you,
>   I will sleep and rest."

"Wait until William has brought thy sherry, *please!*"

"All right now?

> "Moonsilver drowns me deep,
>   I will not call your name,
> I float in the sea of sleep.
> (*God! For those nights of flame!*)"

"Thee needn't look at me that way, Johnnie, I didn't write it. Thee knows thee can say things in poetry that wouldn't do in conversation, and I'm sure it's lovely, they're all lovely, only I hope people won't think they mean anything."

"It must have been very hard to find all the rhymes," Aunt Deborah's faint old voice sighed from the fireside chair that held heaped shawls and a clattering cup and saucer.

"Has thee seen these notices of the dear child's book?" Aunt Susannah pulled them from her knitting-bag. "A clipping bureau sends them to me—did thee ever hear of such a thing? Talbot Towne told me about it. 'Exquisite little songs——' And here's another: 'Reminiscent of Christina Rossetti——' Mm-m! 'Whipped cream and sugared rose leaves——' Thee might throw that one in the fire, Johnnie; it's not worth keeping. Here's one that says 'underlying feeling of spirituality.' I'll leave them here so all of thee can read them."

"How many copies has thee bought, Johnnie?" Aunt Ann asked, suspiciously.

"Oh, plenty," Uncle Johnnie answered, finishing his sherry.

"I don't know where mother's going to put them if she buys any more."

"What's that, Clara?" Aunt Deborah quavered.

24

"I said I didn't know where thee was going to put any more *Stars and Wild Strawberries*, mother. We have them in the attic and in the china closet—even under my bed. I suppose thee's all in the same fix?"

The aunts nodded. Uncle Johnnie walked over to the fireplace and stood balancing from heels to toes, looking at Ophelia over it, floating in her nightgown through a stew of water-lilies, with ghosts of his sisters moving dimly on the glass that covered the painting. What an absurd picture, he thought, and what an art treasure Eliza considers it. With his back to the room he yawned widely. They're off again, he thought, not troubling to separate the excited soft babble into words. Go it, girls!

"Does thee, Johnnie? Johnnie!"

"I beg your pardon, Ann?"

"Does thee think the child should go to New York? Thee knows her heart's set on it. She says people are too good to her here, that she's smothered in comfort and kindness, that she

needs to be lonely in order to write. Wasn't
that it, Sister Eliza?"

"Yes, that was it. But she was so sweet.
She said she was so afraid we'd think she was
ungrateful, or didn't love us enough, but it was
just that she loved us all too much and was too
happy with us, that it kept her from what she
feels is the work she must do."

"She does look on it as a true vocation. Thee
knows I was unalterably opposed to the notion
at first. We all were, weren't we? And what
poor Fred and Amy will do without her I can't
imagine. But I'm beginning to think perhaps
we ought to let her go."

"What does thee think, Johnnie?"

"I've always thought writing could be done
wherever there was a pen and ink and paper,
if you had something to say," Uncle Johnnie
answered.

Aunt Susannah looked at him and closed her
eyes. "Talbot Emery Towne promises to keep
an eye on her," she said. "And thee told me
thy friend's daughter had rooms in a house

26

where Christabel could live, didn't thee, Clara?"

"Adeline Benjamin's daughter—they're *the* Benjamins, thee knows, and before she was married she was one of *the* Boyds. And Christabel and she took to each other when they met. But Fred and Amy thought those rooms were more than they could afford."

"I think it can be managed," Aunt Eliza said, and again the heads nodded, all but Uncle Johnnie's.

"Of course Adeline's daughter is an artist."

"Oh!"

"But still, it's only flowers. I imagine she's a very sweet girl."

"It would be worth more than the extra rent to feel some one was taking care of Christabel."

"I should have thought Christabel could take care of herself," Uncle Johnnie said, and Aunt Ann answered:

"Johnnie, thee always did delight in being perverse."

27

Chapter Three

"WELL," said Boyd Benjamin, leaning in the doorway with her hands in the pockets of her coat, her cigarette wagging to her words, "I must say this place looks exactly like you."

"It *is* nice," Christabel agreed.

"Everything done?"

"Everything but the curtains. Gobby Witherspoon said he'd come in and help me hang them."

"Gobby's having a wonderful time thinking he's in love with you!"

Poor old Boyd, Christabel thought. Imagine having to get one's emotional satisfaction from another woman's love affairs! And she saw herself as she must seem to strong clumsy Boyd—fragile and flower-like, surrounded by adorers; the fairy-tale princess whose glamour poor old Boyd must share, if only in imagination. She answered, warmly gentle:

"He's been perfect to me. You all have. I wonder why?"

"So do I!" Boyd gave her an affectionate blow with a large hand. "You noticed I said *thinking* he's in love with you."

"Yes, I did. I don't think you do Gobby justice, Boyd. I think just because he's so sensitive and because he does things—well, like making these curtains—you don't any of you realize how much depth and strength there is there. Take Elliott Foster, for instance. Gobby's perfectly devoted to Elliott, and I know Elliott thinks Gobby's a light-weight."

"Now Elliott! There's a different matter. There's somebody who really *is* in love with you."

"Oh *no*, Boyd! Nonsense! He isn't at all!"

"All right, you know best. Do you want me to screw the teacup hooks into the cupboard?"

"Thank you. They're—Oh, you've found

them. What in the world makes you have such a *wild* idea? About Elliott, I mean?"

"Oh, nothing."

"No, really, Boyd. He hasn't been near me all week."

"Doesn't that just prove what I'm telling you? He doesn't dare come. He's afraid to admit to himself the way he's feeling. But I saw him looking at you the other day."

"*When* did you?"

"Up in the studio the day you were all there for tea. You went over to the window and said something about the first star, and he sat looking at you as if he was bewitched, and then grabbed his hat and *bolted*. Don't you remember?"

Christabel remembered. She could see the scene as clearly as if she were sitting in the front row of a theatre. The firelight shining on Boyd's paintings of passionate petunias and eggplants of heroic size, Boyd with her short hair and manly clothes leaning against the mantelpiece, a cigarette hanging from the cor-

30

ner of her mouth; gentle Gobby with his turquoise bangle, on a cricket close to the blaze, having one last piece of pastry; Donatia Platt, so affected and arty, all big beads and hammered silver, acting like a fool over Elliott Foster. And Christabel herself in her autumnleaf-brown dress, her face and throat warm ivory in the firelight, outlined against deepening blue. She could even hear her voice saying, "The first star"; she was touched by the sadness in it. Certainly soon after that Elliott had gone, together with the unattractive Platt. At the time it had not seemed significant, but now, in the light of Boyd's words ——

"He's fighting it," said Boyd. "He's afraid you'll interfere with his work. In fact, I don't believe he even knows he's in love with you, yet, but *I* do. Look! Look what's coming! Welcome, little Goblin!"

"Take off my hat for me, Boyd; I haven't a hand. Greetings, Lady Christabel!"

"Unload him, Christabel. Gobby, don't you know it isn't the thing to come through the

31

streets of the great city wrapped in sea-green silk? You might be misunderstood."

"I've had hundreds of little boys following me for blocks. That's your last pair of curtains, Christabel. Here's a pot of car*n*ations, my dear. Did you think you could get them in pots outside of Italy? Put it here by the Della Robbia —— Look, please look at Boyd's expression of suffering! I suppose we seem very old-fashioned and sentimental to her. And, my dears, look at this old copper tray I got from a Russian Jew in Allen Street! You'll always have to sit so that it comes behind your head, like a halo—look! Sweet Saint Christabel!"

"What's in this?"

"Dear Boyd, you're so curious. Cherry tarts, in hopes Christabel will ask me to stay to tea."

"Oh, I do! I ask you both!"

"Can't, thanks. 'By, children."

"How brusque Boyd is," Gobby observed, unwinding a huge pale-blue muffler. "Have

32

you an old newspaper to put on this chair? And if you'll hand me the curtain rod. There's something perfectly ruthless about her—and as for her flower paintings, they frighten me to death. Those obscene calla lilies! Are these folds all right?"

"Just a teeny bit more—*there*. But surely you don't take her paintings seriously, do you, Gobby? Nobody *does*, do they, except, of course, poor darling old Boyd herself? Oh, *oh*, how sweet it looks! The curtains make all the difference in the world!"

"It's a perfect background for you now."

"Is it, Gobby? Am I nice enough for this lovely room? How good you've all been about helping me—I can't imagine why! You, Elliott——"

"Oh, that reminds me—I saw Elliott, and he said he was coming over. He was going to stop at Donatia Platt's first for her book of Beardsley drawings he said he'd promised to lend you!"

"I think he's in love with Donatia."

33

"Well, she's in love with him, and I did think he was with her, sort of; not *crazy*, the way she is, but I always thought Elliott had a mother-fixation, and I thought he'd sort of transferred it to Donatia. Shall I fill the kettle?

The samovar boils on my table of oak
    And my bed with chintz curtains is seen,
Within the dark something the something awoke—"

"What ——?"

"Dostoevski. The Insulted and Injured."

"I wasn't going to say, 'What is it?' I was going to say, 'What a marvelous book it is!' What were we talking about? Oh, Donatia."

"Yes, and Elliott. He really seems to have been avoiding her for the last week or so."

"She's a lovely person."

"Yes, she's a wonderful girl —— look, shall we draw the curtains, or leave them open?"

"Leave them open." And she almost said, "So we can see that first little star, like a silver fish in a deep blue sea," but since Elliott was coming she decided to save it. "But, Gobby,

34

I do feel something about Donatia—you know I have this queer way of feeling people, sometimes I think that's why I get so exhausted. I get simply *limp*, and yet I wouldn't be less sensitive, though one does pay a terrible price. But I do feel something not quite—well, not quite *fine* about her."

"Oh, well, of course she's small-town Middle West. Her name really was Harriet Ruth; she changed it to Donatia to go with her personality. Did Elliott tell you? I think she does pretty well, considering, but naturally compared with *you* ——"

"Oh, now, I don't mean *that* —— come in! Elliott! Just in time, the kettle's boiling, and look! The first star peeping through my sea-green curtains! It's a little silver fish in the deep blue ocean of dusk. See, Elliott. The first star."

"My work must come first, always," said Christabel, as they sat with their empty teacups. And gazing into the fire that leaped and fell, she saw long days packed full of work, she felt herself tingling with work that could be done now that the curtains were up and the teacup hooks screwed in.

Gobby slowly licked cherry juice from his fingers. "Well, I like work myself, sort of —sometimes. That reminds me, don't forget you're posing for me tomorrow. Heavens! I wish some one would get just that turn of the head. Look, Elliott! Don't move, Christabel! Look at that, with the firelight on her cheek and throat—which is she, fire or snow?"

"You make me sound like a Maeterlinck character."

She knew now what to think of Maeterlinck. She had loved him when she lived in Germantown. He had given her unhappy princesses, lost and wailing in the mist, their hair falling about them in shining cascades; graves suddenly blossoming with lilies; velvet bees with soap-bubble-colored wings, flying home to secret golden hives. But since Elliott and

Gobby and Boyd had laughed indulgently and said, "Good old Maeterlinck!" the magus, the keeper of the mysteries, had become the good old prestidigitator, whose most famous trick was to produce from his sleeve a flock of blue-birds that nested in hundreds of Tea Rooms and Gifte Shoppes everywhere.

Barrie was lost to her, too. She had said "Barrie ——" and instantly they had re-sponded:

"Oh, Barrie ——!"

"De*lic*ious Barrie!"

"*Charm*ing Barrie!"

"And now all together, boys and girls! One, two, three ——"

"Whimsical Barrie!"

And she had known she didn't think so much of Barrie. But she must read some—what was it? Dostoevski.

"Only to Give, Give, Give," she wrote in her Secret Journal. "To Sing with a clear shiningness, no matter out of what loneliness and pain, and make the Song the sweeter for

37

the suffering. To feel the happy-hurt of the Beauty-of-Things, and make others feel it. To share the Bread of Beauty through my Work."

Gobby liked that phrase particularly when she showed it to him. He was doing a portrait of her, and so was Elliott. Gobby's, like all his pictures, was made from bits of mirror, carpet fuzz dyed with Easter-egg dyes, and the insides of alarm clocks, but Elliott's was a recognizable Christabel.

As the sittings went on she couldn't help feeling sure that Boyd was right about Elliott loving her. When she thought of Donatia Platt there was a warm, breathless lightness in her chest instead of the clenched heaviness she had felt before. She went out of her way to see Donatia now, to praise her to Elliott, who answered absent-mindedly. And when people reported catty remarks made about her by Donatia, she tried only to pity her.

She was getting ready to go to Donatia's one afternoon when Gobby arrived.

"I'm taking her over some things for her

38

party tonight. You can help me carry them.
My wine-glasses, and that bunch of calendulas.
I thought they'd go with her orange curtains."

"Oh, Christabel, you're awfully sweet,
but ——"

"But what, Gobby?"

"Well—let *me* take them. Don't you
bother."

"Nonsense! Why shouldn't I go?"

"Well, you're too sweet and loving to understand, but I think maybe—well, I mean,
you know how Donatia feels about Elliott, and
how Elliott feels about you ——"

"What perfect nonsense!"

"Oh, I know! You have to be told a thousand times before you believe anyone l—likes
you. But Donatia knows how Elliott feels, if
you don't. Well, to tell you the truth, though
I haven't any business to, I've just been there
and she was crying, and she sort of burst out
about how she wished she was dead ——"

"Oh, poor girl! I must hurry to her! You're

mistaken, Gobby. It's Donatia Elliott loves. He doesn't love me." She pulled on her embroidered cap before the mirror, fluffing out dark auburn tendrils over her ears, looking deep into her own shining eyes. "I don't say that he didn't think he was—well, crazy about me for a little while, but of *course* I had to stop that, knowing how Donatia felt, and that's why the way she's acting now does hurt me a little, when I've done everything to try to make Elliott appreciate her. I wouldn't say this to anyone in the world but you, Gobby, but Donatia hasn't been very kind to me, and *so* I must love her just twice as hard, don't you see?"

Donatia's eyes were red and her voice hard when Christabel and Gobby came in with their offerings, but that evening she was blazing with laughter and excitement. What *does* Elliott see in her? Christabel thought, watching them together. Make-up just plastered on—and her voice when she gets excited! Donatia, indeed!

40

Harriet Ruth Platt. The clenched tightness came back in her chest. She called:

"Elliott! Come here a minute!" And then: "Oh, Donatia *darling!* Were you talking to him? I didn't notice! *Keep* him!"

Will he come? she thought, will he come? And her whole being willed, Come, so intensely that she felt weak with relief when he said, "Excuse me a minute, Donatia," and came across the room.

She began to talk wildly to anybody, everybody but Elliott, hearing her own voice as if it belonged to some one else, glowing from the admiring laughter that broke over her words. "She's turned the hostess into an innocent bystander," she heard a girl whisper; but the man she whispered to only answered, "Did you hear what that was she said?"

"What did you say those mandarin oranges were, Christabel?"

"Mandarin oranges are Chinese emperors. Fat little men in imperial yellow crêpe, with their hands tucked into their sleeves."

41

"What are the grapes? Ask her what the grapes are."

"Oh, the grapes are the emperors' smooth little concubines in their robes of water-green silk."

"Let's be emperors and concubines! Let's dress up!"

"I speak for the sofa cover!"

"I choose that batik!"

"I have an idea. Where's your white scarf with the gold embroidery, Donatia? You know, that one I gave you?"

"Here it is, Elliott! What are you going to be?"

"I want it for Christabel. Here, let me bind it tight around your head and under your chin. Cross your hands, this way. My God! Look, everybody! Look! Did you ever see such a marvelous mediæval Madonna?"

"She must be in a shrine. Here, lift her up on the table! Give us the flowers, Donatia, and look—put the candles around her. On your knees, worshipers!"

42

"I'll never forget you with that white-and-gold thing round your head," Elliott told Christabel, taking her home. "You've never looked so lovely. Listen! Why don't we go back and borrow it from Donatia and you come over tomorrow morning and let me do a sketch of you? Come on!"

"Oh, we can't go back *now*!"

"Why not? We haven't been gone five minutes. She won't be in bed or anything."

"I don't think she'll want to lend it to me."

"She'll love to lend it to you."

"I'm afraid not. I wouldn't say this to anyone in the world but you, Elliott, but Donatia hasn't been very kind to me."

"Now you're doing her an injustice. You feel things that aren't intended, you're so sensitive and tender-hearted."

"Do I, Elliott? Perhaps you're right. Perhaps I am unjust to her. Anyway, I feel that you're a very understanding person, and if you say so, we'll go back."

Donatia's face was scarlet as she opened the

door to them, and the room was filled with a smell of burning. "My scarf? Yes, of course." She looked around the room, and Christabel looked, too. Candle grease, grape skins, a macaroon crushed into the rug, Gobby's blue muffler left behind. "Some one must have gone off with it. It isn't here."

Christabel looked only once at the filmy charred rag of white and gold in the fireplace. She threw her arms around Donatia and kissed her scorched cheek, crying, "You've given us a *heavenly* evening!" before she ran—floated—flew down the stairs, hand in hand with Elliott.

Chapter Four

CHRISTABEL wrote in her Secret Journal:
"Let me work at white heat, let me be molten in the flame!

"What is anything in comparison with this lonely shining Joy of Creation? This welling of the water from the deep below the deep, this blessed privilege of being the cup to hold the water that brims over for the thirsty? Nothing must interfere with my work, no thoughts of self, no selfish joy or sorrow. The bees have flown far, in orchards and meadows. Now I call them back to the hive, and in darkness and silence they make the golden honey.

"Oh, Passion of Work, fill me and flood me! Is there a World? I forget."

She had inked her finger, so she washed her hands and rubbed cold cream into them, looking at them critically. Elliott said her hands made him believe in God. She tried them in different positions.

Well, now to work.

First she cleared her desk of the quill in its glass of shot, the snowstorm paperweight Gobby had found for her, her mother's latest letter, Mrs. Talbot Emery Towne's invitation to Sunday luncheon, an invitation to read from her poems at the Saturday Salon, and a note from Elliott, which she reread, glowing pleasantly. Then she sharpened a handful of pencils and put them in a row by a pile of yellow paper.

If she didn't answer Mrs. Towne's invitation before she began to work, it would be a gnat in her mind. And that Salon thing. She wrote the notes. What should she wear when she read her poems? In spite of the dirty snow, it was too near spring for velvet. Her blue dress with lace collar and cuffs? That made her look like a demure child. She was going to read the three unpublished poems that made up "Love on the Mesa." "Vermillion paint and slanting eagle feather," "The yellow cactus bloomed for us today," and "Death coiled and rattling in the blue rock shadow." She could

46

see herself, hear herself, hear her audience. How has that child lived long enough to have felt so deeply, to have suffered so?

The earth in her pot of hyacinths was hard and gray. White hyacinths to feed the soul. She watered it, watching the water bubble up through the cracks. She yawned.

Now to work.

She was writing a romance of old Spain, called *Carnation Flower*. "Chapter Eight," she wrote, and gazed at the words. Then she drew three lines under them and yawned again.

Now what? Annunciata had to be gotten to the bull-fight, but how to get her there? A true artist never wrote:

"Chapter Eight.

"Annunciata went to the bull-fight to see Juan ——" though that was what must be conveyed.

How to begin the chapter? She pulled book after book from her shelves and dipped in to see how other authors did. Dostoevski, Hardy,

47

James. She would sit at the feet of the masters.

"Two days after the incident I have described I met her ——"

"On an early winter afternoon, clear but not cold, when the vegetable world was a weird multitude of skeletons ——"

"It will probably not surprise the reflective reader ——"

Somehow they were not helpful. Lesser lights might show the path.

"'Enery,' said Mrs. Hawkins, severely, as the cutlets sputtered in the pan ——"

"Corinthia sat in her coach, her cheeks glowing faintly, her full skirts drifting like snow about her ——"

Christabel tumbled the books back into their places, and wrote quickly:

"Annunciata sat in her box, her skin glowing faintly with the patina of pale old gold, a snowfall of white lace drifting across hair that reflected the light like black water. She was in white except for the red rose, deep as velvet,

48

that held the mantilla to the extravagant comb, and the great fan, painted with death and glory, that hid the passionate beating of her heart. The dark eyes curtained by proud lids, the beautiful scornful mouth, the languid hand unfurling the fan, were calm, but as Juan ran into the bull ring she was a flame wrapped in snow."

Then she stopped again.

How could she write about passion until she had felt it in more than the general way all artists feel everything? Didn't she owe it to her art to live more fully? She had been thinking so, off and on, all winter, and now spring made her sure. These conventions, these old taboos! Chains to a soul that longed for freedom, chains that one touch of truth and courage would break.

She knew Elliott loved her. That he had never told her so in words only made her more certain, especially after talks with Boyd Benjamin, full of thrilling psychological explanations. Chiefly, Boyd said, he was afraid of

49

admitting his passion because it might interfere with his work. Interfere! Christabel
laughed with tender mockery. It would re-
lease the floods of artistic creation in him as
well as in her. We will be together on the
mountain tops, my dearest. You and I together, and the world forgotten. We will
know the deepest and the highest, we will know
heart-piercing reality.

No use in hesitating, now that she had decided. "Oh, at last!" she whispered to herself as she stepped out of her clothes and into
her best chemise. Her hands were snow
against her flaming cheeks. She went over to
her desk and read the last words she had
written. "She was a flame wrapped in snow."

How her heart was pounding! She patted
Lilas blanc behind her ears and got out fresh
gloves. The slushy snow made galoshes necessary. That was annoying.

At the door she paused and covered her face
with her hands. "Oh, my dear, be very gentle
to me," she whispered.

Elliott's door was unlocked, but his room was empty. It had always been set in order for company when she had visited it, and the way it looked now was a surprise. A cat and a loaf of bread lay in his unmade bed, assorted objects on the floor had to be stepped over, obscene pictures were drawn with red chalk on the walls. Christabel looked at them, feeling how astonishing it was that she, brought up as she had been, could be so broad-minded and tolerant about them, could even admire the cleverness of their execution.

She shook her head with a little motherly, smiling sigh. She gathered up boots, paint-rags, and a frying-pan with bits of egg still stuck in it, and pushed them behind a bulging curtain. She took his best silk muffler, hanging over a chair back, to dust with, and then threw it after the boots and frying-pan. The sheets went, too. The curtain bulged like a sail in a storm.

She saw herself and Elliott in varied striking tableaux. She saw him kneeling, kissing the

51

hem of her skirt. "My little saint! My little shining saint!" She felt his arms about her; his kisses closed her eyes. Oh, my dear, be very gentle to me!

She set the kettle to boil, and lit the candles on either side of the primroses she had brought him. "Blessed!" she said aloud, and kissed them. Shining pale yellow in the candlelight, symbols of innocent gentleness. The time she had had getting them! The clerk had been a perfect fool, and she had told him just what she thought when he had tried to make her take the ordinary mauve ones.

She had meant to have Elliott come, tired and lonely out of the cold, to find her there with her great grave gift of love and understanding and peace. Three accompanying gentlemen had been no part of her plan. But there they were, looking more startled than she felt, for their conversation on the stairs had been loud and unstudied.

They got tea jerkily behind another curtain; she heard their agitated murmurs and smelled scorching toast. Then came the sound of scraping. But she prudently refused the dingy slices, remembering where the loaf had lain.

There was a chair for Christabel. The others sat on the floor at her feet. Elliott, Peabody Baxter, whose drawings sometimes appeared in *The Dial*, a Russian model, and a timid youth who kept on a large muffler throughout for fear his collar was not clean enough for this radiant being.

The Russian understood no English, but turned his face to each speaker, his mouth full of scorched toast, his childlike eyes shining happily.

"Isn't it dreadfully sloppy?"

"Dreadfully! The penalty of spring is slush."

"Did you notice my primroses, Elliott? They make me feel four years old again, with apple cheeks and a fresh white pinny."

If there had been no primroses in her childhood, there were plenty in the Kate Greenaway books that she had almost succeeded in forget-

53

ting were fairly recent purchases, the books on whose fly-leaves she had written Christabel Caine in large childish letters.

"Spring in England——"

"Oh! Primroses in the hedges—wet primroses with tall pink stems and crisp ruffled leaves!"

She could hear her voice, charming, with a little breathless catch in it now and then. She did not so much think, I am like a primrose, as hope some of the gentlemen were thinking it. Like a primrose, innocently gay, fresh, touching——

She outstayed the others. Even Elliott's nervous offers to take her home had no effect.

"Don't send me away, my dear. I have something I must say to you. Help me!"

"I certainly will, if you'll tell me——"

"It is so foolishly hard! And I ought to be able to say it as easily, as simply, as a bird sings, as those primroses bloom."

"I——"

54

"I won't be so silly, so frightened! Elliott! I have seen everything!"

"I—uh—uh ——"

"You have been wonderful in your silence, and I know it was because you were afraid of startling me, shocking me, wasn't it? Don't think I didn't understand, and love you for it. But one doesn't need words for the greatest things, I think, and I have understood your wordless message, dear. You *do* care for me a little, don't you?"

"Oh, I should say I do! Why, I really practically—worship you. You know I do, Christabel! I sort of feel—well, religious, when I'm with you ——"

"Love *is* religion, I think. But don't make a saint of me, my dear. I'm just a woman who needs her lover's arms."

She waited for him to answer, but he remained silent and motionless, gazing at her with an expression of adoring horror, so she went on.

55

"Can't we speak to each other *truly?* Must there be this barrier of pretense between us?"

"Oh, Christabel, of course! I mean, of course *not*—I mean ——"

"I have come to you. Do you understand? Will you take my gift?"

He knelt before her. His head went down in her lap. She bent above him tenderly; she stroked his hair with a hand she couldn't keep from shaking.

"Look at me, my lover!"

"Do you mean—Christabel! Do you mean you'll be engaged to me?"

Well, perhaps it's better, she thought, relieved and disappointed, as she received his reverent kiss. Because, after all, one must think of others. Mother and father, the aunts. Love isn't true love if it makes us selfish. A cloud of white satin and tulle floated through her mind, trailing a fragrance of orange-blossoms. Poor Gerald Smith. I, Christabel, take thee, Elliott —— Yes, this was better.

While her hand, steady now, still stroked his

56

hair, she shifted her position, for the chair was beginning to get a little hard. What is he thinking about? she wondered. Should she carry lilies, or a prayer-book? Donatia Platt in an orange smock blotted out the gleaming vision of herself in her wedding dress, and the phrase popped into her mind, she didn't know why, Sacred and Profane Love.

What are you thinking about, my darling? What words can I find that are beautiful enough to break this beautiful silence between us?

Chapter Five

"I'LL face any sacrifice with you gladly—oh, *glad*ly!" Christabel told Elliott. "I know life isn't going to be easy for us, darling, but what does anything matter as long as we have each other? And I want you to promise not to mind my family if it doesn't quite understand. You see, it's a darling family, but it loves me a little bit *too* much; it has silly ideas about me, and so, though you're the most wonderful man in the world, the dear geese aren't going to think even you are good enough for their marvelous, wonderful Christabel!"

"Well, they won't be so very far wrong. I——"

She put a hand across his mouth and he kissed it, thinking again, how good it smells! How can I ever be worthy of her? If I could only make her happy. But her eyes had an other-world look in them; she spoke of sacrifice so often, beautifully, he thought, but sadly.

After all, getting married wasn't entirely sacrifice. Some people seemed to enjoy parts of it, at least. But Christabel, with her shining eyes and gallant words, sometimes made him feel as if he had helped her into the tumbril and started her off toward the guillotine.

There can be sacrifice on both sides, he thought. It's not going to be so easy to paint the things I want to paint, with a wife to support.

"We're never going to interfere with each other's work," she said.

"Well, but the kind of thing I do now isn't bringing in enough to live on."

"Dearest, I *know* you can find other things, just to do in your spare time. You see, you don't realize how wonderful you are, and I *do!* I be*lieve* in you, Elliott!"

"What sort of things?"

"Oh, cover designs and things like that."

"I loathe the idea!"

She looked wounded.

"Of course I'd do anything to make our marriage possible, but that sort of thing is simply soul-destroying."

"I don't see why. Think of the people you could reach, the good you could do!"

"I'm trying to do serious work, Christabel. I can't do popular stuff. I ———"

"My dear, don't I *know!* I'm just the same; I couldn't bear it if people in general liked my writing. If you speak as truly as you can, and as beautifully, refusing to shriek and scream and get easy effects, how can you expect to be heard through all the noise of bad popular writing?"

"What I mean about my painting ———"

"Painting isn't writing, Elliott. Of *course* you must go on with your real work, but you could *eas*ily do other things just for relaxation. Why, look at some of the advertisements! Beautiful! And they pay tre*men*dously!"

"You don't understand."

"Oh, Elliott! How you hurt me!"

And then he had to comfort her, tell her she did understand, always, ask for her forgiveness.

He might as well get to work on canned peaches and silk stockings, he thought, for he was so upset most of the time now that he couldn't concentrate on decent painting. But he hugged to himself for comfort the thought that theirs was a great love, and the greater the love the greater the suffering, according to the classics. And he must be loyal to her, even if he didn't want to be—but he did, he did! He loved her as no woman had ever been loved before, he assured himself. And he must be as loyal as she who promised him so sweetly:

"Nothing the family can say will ever change me."

So he had expected her family to despise him. Not that I care, he thought, in the train on his way to be inspected, sustaining himself by the memory of the still life of calla lilies he was painting. Let them despise me! I despise them! I care less than nothing what anyone in the world thinks of me, except Christabel. He moved his head up and down to ease the pain in the back of his neck, and looked

61

at his new mauve shirt and dark purple tie in
the glass of the train window.

But now, sitting with Uncle Johnnie after
dinner at Aunt Deborah's, on the last evening
of his Germantown visit, he knew the family
considered him a nice young man. They
beamed approval, they had offered an allow-
ance, a little house to be built in a corner of
Shady Lawn, a position in Cousin William
Starkweather's advertising business, with a sal-
ary that would make living easy. He had
been completely accepted as one of them on the
day when Aunt Eliza took him for a drive and
showed him the spot in the cemetery where he
would be buried. She had been so pleased
about it, and had so glowingly described the
beauty of the dogwood there in the spring—
"You'll enjoy that, with your artistic eye"—
that he had felt his faltered thanks to be inadequate.

But I'll do whatever they want me to do, for
Christabel's sake, he decided. The calla lilies
that had comforted him at first had grown

fainter and fainter through the week—now they floated between him and the butler bringing in coffee, and faded away completely. I'd give anything to make her happy, he thought, and made himself remember the way she had looked coming downstairs tonight in her white dress, the quick handclasp she had given him as she left him alone with Uncle Johnnie.

"Thank you, sir," he said, taking a cigar he didn't want. He felt faint with fatigue. All week he had been lost in a regiment of old women, picking up balls of wool, drinking rivers of tea, trotting for miles through conservatories full of rare plants, waxen or hairy, while he agreed with voices flung briskly back or quavering feebly from bundles of shawls, saying that Christabel was a wonderful person. Shady Lawn, The Cedars, Ferncroft. Great-aunts Deborah, Eliza, Lydia, Hannah, Susannah, and Ann. They melted from one to another in his mind, figures in a fever-dream. Cups of tea, balls of wool, hairy, spiny, waxen plants, and his mouth aching from its constant stretch of nervous smile.

Being engaged was marvelous, of course, but it was exhausting. Emotion took it out of one, and having to be intense and real all the time. The room was hot and made his head swim—or was it the cigar?

"Here, have another drop of brandy," said Uncle Johnnie.

Elliott for one wild moment wanted to put his head down on Uncle Johnnie's shoulder and burst into tears. He wanted to say, "How have you managed to keep free among them all?" But the butler opened a window and the brandy spread through him reassuringly. Once more he was himself, the happiest man in the world, except for the knowledge that he could never be worthy of the wonderful girl he was engaged to.

Mr. Caine was in bed with a cold, and Mrs. Caine went upstairs early, with elaborate yawns. Christabel and Elliott stood gazing into the fire. He was remembering some ad-

64

vice Uncle Johnnie had given him that evening. "Don't be so reverent with her. Women like men to be rough." He thought of a brainless athlete named Gerald Smith, all bulging muscles and curly yellow excelsior for hair, who seemed to enchant Christabel by snatching her at parties they had been to, and dancing her off with never a question as to whether he might have the pleasure. And suddenly Elliott threw his arms around Christabel and pulled her down on the sofa with such force that it surprised them both. But then, once he had kissed her, he wasn't sure he knew how to go on being just rough enough. Besides, he felt too tired tonight. He slid down to the floor, his head against her knees, and she began to stroke his hair. It made him feel sleepy, and before he could stop himself he gave a loud gasping yawn.

She pushed his head impatiently and he twisted around and gazed up at her.

"What's the matter, darling?"

"Oh, nothing." Her sigh was almost a sob.

He searched his mind for something to please her.

"I was just thinking how wonderful it was to sit here together in silence, and yet each of us knowing everything the other was thinking and feeling."

But it was no good. He saw one of her moods coming over her as clearly as he had seen the bright fluidity of water dull and harden in freezing cold. Moods called by Christabel herself, as he had read in her Secret Journal, "those dark cold tides that drown me." He tried again, apprehensively:

"You look so beautiful in this dim light."

It did not need the sound that from anyone else he would have called a snort, to tell him that could have been better. He hurried on:

"I'm always afraid of being too rough with you—of shattering something exquisite by a touch or a word when you look the way you're looking now."

She relaxed enough to lay her hand on him lightly, as if in accolade.

66

"I always feel like that place in *Carnation Flower* where Juan has a fever and goes into the church and thinks the Madonna is Annunciata."

"Juan and Annunciata! Elliott, am I betraying them? Am I silly? Tell me I am! I have this feeling that when *Carnation Flower* is published, if it is published——"

"*If!*"

"Well, then, *when*—I have this feeling that they'll feel betrayed. I've made them from bits of my own heart, my dreams, my secret things, and it seems wrong, somehow, to show them just to anybody, to *sell* them."

"Think of the good you'll be doing."

"How do you mean?"

"Well, bringing such beauty into the world, and—I don't know—I mean—such truth——"

"Well, I *do* think that—hope it, anyway. My poor little book may not have very much, but I have tried to give it truth and beauty. But don't be disappointed in me when it isn't popular, darling. Will you promise? Because it won't be. I don't want it to be. I want just to speak simply, truly, to the few who will understand. You know I don't want what the world means when it says success ———"

"Oh, I *do* know, darling. That's just the way I feel about my own work."

"*What* do I write for, Elliott? Not for success. I should feel sick with terror if that came to me. I'd know I'd failed, somehow, that I hadn't been true to the *real* things. Not for pleasure, *cer*tainly, for my work is done in grief and pain, and I don't use those words lightly, dear. And yet I must write or die. Why is this burden on me?"

"Because you have the artist's soul, Christabel. I know how it is myself ———"

"Will I never go free?"

"Never, my darling."

"Will I always have to suffer this ache of beauty? Oh, Elliott, will I always have to suffer?"

Oh, beautiful girl! his heart cried, worship-

68

ing the glowing face she bent above him. And
she loves me. Not Gerald Smith, not anyone
else in the world. She loves me. She might
have chosen anyone, she's so popular at every
party; everyone loves her, but she loves me.
The foot he was sitting on began to go to sleep,
but he tried to keep from moving, for fear of
shattering their perfect moment.

Chapter Six

CHRISTABEL'S engagement had helped her work so much that *Carnation Flower*, published that spring, was quite a success. But by the time it was in the bookshops she was glad to go to Atlantic City for a rest, with Aunt Lydia, who wanted company.

Aunt Lydia was as good as Talbot Emery Towne's whole publicity department. She advertised Christabel and *Carnation Flower* to all the old ladies and gentlemen in the combined hotel and sanitarium where she and Christabel stayed; she dealt out copies to those who could not be bullied into buying. She went up and down the Boardwalk in a rolling-chair, asking for *Carnation Flower* at all the bookshops. The inmates of Oversea Hall were well trained by her. They waited about with *Carnation Flowers* and fountain pens, to ask for autographs, they broke off talk of health to talk literature with the authoress. "Have you read

that lovely new book by Zona Grey? Or is
it by Zane Gale? Fiddlesticks! I always get
those two mixed up!"

Christabel was sweet to them all. "But I
wish they wouldn't treat us quite so much like
royalty!" she complained whimsically to Aunt
Lydia. "You and Mrs. Carey are so regal
that even I become a princess in your reflected
glory, Aunt Lydia darling!"

"Thee's an absurd child," Aunt Lydia answered, fondly. They were dining at a table
covered with little dishes of this and that, with
library paste for sauce. At the next table old
Mr. Blanchard was having both vanilla ice-
cream and a Boston cream puff, and Mrs.
Blanchard was sneaking an apple into her knitting-bag. I hope age brings me something
more beautiful than greediness, Christabel
thought, watching them. I hope it brings me
even deeper love and understanding.

In the doorway the headwaitress stretched
her mouth to show her teeth to arriving and de-
parting diners, and then followed them with

71

cold eyes. What a place, Christabel thought, trying first a kiss full of shredded string cocoa-nut, then a sawdust lady-finger.

Mrs. Carey sailed out, making the signals of head and hand that meant "See you outside," and Aunt Lydia fluttered her fingers. Then came the Simpsons, who, because they had bought a copy of *Carnation Flower*, were inclined to presume. Mrs. Simpson tottering on too high heels, a mountain of black lace with a crimson rose on the lower slopes, bowed impressively, and so did gray-coated, white-trousered Mr. Simpson. Aunt Lydia dealt them a small cold unsmiling bow.

"Thee knows, I think that woman's hair is dyed. And so pushing—just because thee wrote in thy book for them they'll be telling people thee's a friend of theirs. Thee'll see! Through, dear? I suppose Mrs. Carey will be waiting."

They in their turn were affable to the head-waitress. They went through the reception hall, and on past the room where a little dark man peeped out from his store of gauze scarfs and knitting-bags, a little dark man, Christabel thought, who should have worn a turban and looked out from another bazaar on bare feet, yashmaks, camels swaying past, instead of on fat ladies, old gentlemen thin and trembling as dead leaves, and black boys drifting by with pitchers of ice-water. He'll never know, she thought, what I have felt about him. And yet it all helps. Every understanding thought, every kind thought, helps—somehow.

Mrs. Carey with two lesser ladies was already at the card table that was reserved for her and for Aunt Lydia night after night, and bridge began.

"Your bid, Lady."

"*My* bid? Mercy! what a hand!"

"Don't expect any help from me, partner!"

"Mustn't talk across the table, ladies."

"'Scuse us, please? Us was naughty dirls, but us'll be dood now!"

"Try one of these chocolates in silver paper, Mrs. Huntington."

"Thee's a bad lady, to tempt me!"

"I just wish chocolates liked me as well as I like them!"

"Have a chocolate, Christabel dear? I must get rid of these before my son comes tomorrow, or he'll think I didn't appreciate them."

"Is thy son coming tomorrow?"

"Yes. Isn't it wonderful that he's able to get down again so soon. *Mm!* Mershy! B'carefu' thish kin'—mmp! Cologne or something inside these big round ones!" She buried her chin in her breast, as a pigeon buries its bill. "Did I spill? I guess not. Yes, Curtis is coming. I was so surprised when he wrote that he'd be down this week, too."

Christabel, sharing a chair beside the bridge table with Aunt Lydia's book and shawl and work-bag, saw through a shining mist the roomful of old ladies, pale or purple, playing bridge

74

by the light of mustard-shaded lamps. She, too, had received a letter from Mrs. Carey's son saying he was coming again to Atlantic City, but she was not surprised.

She had been thinking of Curtis Carey 3d a great deal since his visit last week to Oversea Hall. She liked to make excuses to say his name. "Who told me that? Oh, I know—it was Curtis Carey." "Curtis Carey says his mother says you're one of the few real aristocrats she knows, Aunt Lydia." "Curtis Carey——"

She was planning to write a new book for his eyes, as *Carnation Flower* had been written for Elliott's. It must show him the depth and beauty of her nature; it must show him, subtly, how used she was to things like footmen and conservatories, and how little they impressed her.

Sometimes Curtis and Elliott would come into her mind side by side, not to Elliott's advantage. The thought of him made her feel wise and sad and subtle, made her feel old as

75

the stars or the sea. It was at one of those times that she wrote the poem beginning:

> The age-old pain of a woman's heart—
> The age-old sob of the sea—

But he loves me so! she would think. He will be happy, and I will have my work, and, after all, life isn't so terribly long, and then comes peace. But when it was Curtis she thought of, she wrote to Elliott. The more glowing her thoughts of the one, the more intense her letters to the other. It was unfortunate that just at this time Elliott had sprained his right wrist so that he could only write a few jerky and tremulous lines with his left hand, or dictate restrainedly to Gobby.

OH, MY HEART'S DEAREST! [she wrote to Elliott, with a hand that shook as she thought of Curtis, who had arrived that day]

How I miss—*miss* you! When will the Wings stir in my heart again? I'm like a prism that is nothing until the Sun shines through it, and wakes it up, and makes it laugh and sparkle and scatter Shreds of Rainbow all about—and you're the Sun! I need you, Sun of my Heart!

This place is so dreary, my darling. It's a temptation to let one's little shining be buried under Talk of Health and Knitted Shawls and Diets and Draughts. But then I think, here are poor sick old things being brave enough to put on their beads and tell jokes, and outside are the Sky and the Sea. And I try to shine for them, gently, until they shine back at me. They love me, Elliott—isn't it touching? It makes me feel so humble.

And I *am* happy, Dearest. Isn't there a You? I went down on the sand yesterday at sunset, under a pink sky, with a pink and green sea, foam-edged, creeping up to my feet. And I sent you a message by a small Rosy Cloud —did it reach you? And I thought, here am I, ungrateful one, being unhappy in a World where there are Waves and Courage and Work

to be Done and Little Pink Clouds and My
Own Dear—and all my discouragements left
me, and the Round World sang!

Forever and forever,
CHRISTABEL.

She put her letter into an envelope, took it
out again, and got her Secret Journal. Curtis
Carey and she were going for a walk and he
would be waiting for her, but it was better to
let him wait a few minutes. She began to
copy, the letters growing more and more scal-
loped through her agitation at the thought of
Curtis:

"This place is so dreary—it's a temptation
to let one's little shining be buried under Talk
of Health and Knitted Shawls and Diets ——"

"I was afraid you'd forgotten about me,"
Curtis said, as she stepped out of the elevator.

"Oh, did I keep you waiting? I didn't mean
to. I'm *so* sorry! And such a place to wait
in! Lost in a jungle of potted palms, among
these big chairs like a herd of elephants."

"You certainly can express things wonderfully!"

"Oh no! But I do try to see the funny side of things. It helps, I think. Don't you?"

"Yes, indeed. There's nothing like a sense of humor."

"No, is there?"

"I'm always sorry for people who haven't any."

"*Aren't* you?"

This sedate conversation was getting them nowhere. It had been different in her anticipation. But she was sustained, as they went along the Boardwalk, by the knowledge that they were a good-looking couple. She felt that to deny one's own good looks was both silly and ungrateful. She had written in her Journal:

"It isn't Outer Beauty that I want, and yet I must be grateful for this gift that makes me able to give pleasure to so many. And I can't help knowing that some kind people think I'm lovely-looking. I can't put my fingers in my

79

ears and shut my eyes *all* the time. But I want to be both grateful for it and humble about it, so I have made myself this little prayer:

"Oh, Lord, I thank Thee for Thy Gift of Beauty, but I pray Thee to let my body be only the Cloud that thinly veils the Real Beauty within. And, if Thou wilt, let that grow brighter and more bright, until it shines through this Cloud of my body. Amen."

And Curtis Carey's clothes were enough to make the world a better-looking place, even if they had not contained Curtis. His expensive hat, set on one side of his head, was enchanting to Christabel after the Oversea Hall atmosphere, so lacking in dash. As she looked at it she thought of Elliott, with his hair always a little too long, in a fringe in the back.

"I read your book last week. It's great!"

"Oh, *do* you like it, really? Thank you *so* much!"

"Gosh! I don't see how you can think of it all. And then writing it all out!"

"It's the thing I love to do."

"It sort of scared me about coming down again. I was afraid I couldn't be high-brow enough to interest you."

"*You!* When I've been thinking all week that you'd never want to talk to me again after I'd shown you how ignorant I am!"

"*You* ignorant!"

"Yes. I don't know anything about all the things you know everything about—salmon fishing, and yachting, and being in China, and riding to hounds ——"

She felt herself growing younger by the minute. He knows so much, she thought. He is so strong. I'm nothing but a child compared with him. Helpless. But strongly, tenderly protected.

"Well, but, Good Lord! those are just things I've happened to do. It isn't like having wonderful thoughts, like yours."

"You see, we've always been poor, and I've lived so simply. We have a little bit of a house, and there's just mother and father and me, with our funny old Katie Sullivan to take care of us, and love me and order me about just as if I were a little girl still, and then there's our little garden—I do adore that so! You see, the gentleman we call in moments of grandeur the gardener is also furnace man and window-washer and everything, so I take care of the flowers. And the furniture's shabby and my dresses are made over, but I'm such a goose that as long as there's a rose to smell or a poem to read I don't know enough not to be happy!"

"You know, you're a wonderful girl! I mean, most of the girls I know would sort of put on and try to make an impression—I mean, they wouldn't be just sweet and sincere, the way you are."

"Oh, but what else *could* one be? What else except sincere, I mean? Because, after all, being real is the only thing that matters, isn't it? To be really real and to be kind."

"Well, you're both, all right! I saw last week the way you acted with mother and Mrs. Huntington, and believe me, I know it isn't

82

always easy to be so sympathetic and consider-
ate with older people."

"Do you know, you're rather an—understanding—person?"

"Were you surprised when I wrote that I
was coming down again?"

"Surprised isn't the word!"

"Were you sorry?"

She answered with a glance.

"I broke a date to go to the National with a
foursome this week-end."

"Oh, *why* did you?"

"Can't you guess?"

"Because you knew how happy it would
make your mother to have you come here, I
think. Isn't it touching? Doesn't it make
your heart *ache*, to think how happy we can
make them? Oversea Hall seems so dreary
sometimes, it's a temptation to let oneself be
buried under talk about health and diets and
draughts and shawls; and then I think of their
being old, and yet brave enough to dress up
and make little jokes—it makes me want to

83

cry, it makes me want to do something beautiful for them ——"

"When you talk like that you make me feel
like—don't think I'm silly or sentimental or
anything, but—well, like saying my prayers to
you."

She looked at him gently. There were tears
in her eyes. For her, too, waited that black pit
of age, at the end of the long road, the road of
renunciation that she must travel because of
her promise to Elliott. She looked through her
tears at this understanding man who had never
heard of Elliott.

"But I didn't come to see mother. I came
to see you."

"I'm glad," she said, simply, with a smile
that made him flush, a touch of her hand on
his, lighter than a butterfly.

They played bridge with Mrs. Carey and
Aunt Lydia after dinner. Christabel, being
exquisitely kind to the old, hardly looked at
Curtis, but she felt his eyes on her all evening.

84

She fell asleep thinking of him, thrilling in the dark.

In the gray of the morning she was wakened by Aunt Lydia's maid. Aunt Deborah was dangerously ill. They were to leave at once.

All the way to Philadelphia Christabel fretted. If only she had known yesterday ——

But a letter came from Curtis:

"What have I done? Why did you run away without a word? If I come over to Germantown next Saturday, will you see me?"

And the following Monday Christabel wrote to Elliott:

"Let me go from your life with no bitterness, no crying-out, but gently, as the Little Mermaid melted into foam. We have always given each other Truth, and I must give you Truth now, although it breaks my heart ——" And so strong is habit that she ended the sentence "my darling," and had to rewrite the letter.

Chapter Seven

Elliott answered Christabel's letter beautifully. Then he lay down, at eleven o'clock in the morning, and slept until Gobby came in and stepped on the cat at seven that evening.

The two men had supper together at The Mouse Trap. Elliott found it pleasant to be back in the familiar atmosphere of orange curtains, candle drippings, and sprays of bittersweet, with Lola and Peggy friendly and welcoming, slapping around in their sandals, after all the small dark Italian restaurants he had been to lately. Christabel had not seemed to care for the various tearooms, run by awfully nice girls, that he had patronized before his engagement.

As they ate their chicken patties and icecream, he explained to Gobby that his life was in pieces and that he couldn't talk about it yet.

"Now listen, Elliott, what you've got to do

is to get to work on your painting. How long since you've done anything?"

"Well, not since we—not since Christabel —we —— I've been too busy living, Gobby. And now that I'll have the time, what's the use?"

"Make her sorry."

"I wouldn't do anything in the world to cause her pain."

"All the same, I do think you ought to get back to your painting. Sublimate your emotion, man!"

"It's easy to talk, but you haven't lost everything that makes life worth while," Elliott answered, mournfully, his eyes fixed on the gigantic slice of chocolate cake crumbling beneath his fork.

"I'd rather have your memories than most people's realizations."

"Yes, nothing can take those from me. Somehow I knew this would happen. I knew it was all too perfect to come true. What had I to offer a wonderful girl like Christabel? And

87

yet like a fool I went on hoping—deceiving myself."

"Well, think of Abélard and Héloïse, and Dante and Beatrice—they were always getting separated or something, and they're the world's great lovers. Tristram and Isolde, too— Romeo and Juliet——"

Elliott and Christabel. Elliott just stopped himself from saying it aloud. Mr. Foster and Miss Caine. How different that sounded! But Elliott and Christabel——

"You'd never be satisfied, either of you, with bourgeois contentment. I don't so much mean make her sorry as I mean make her proud of you. Demi-tasse? I think we'd better have big cups of coffee tonight, don't you? With cream?"

"I don't care—yes, cream. It all seems so empty."

"Big cups, Peggy, please. Of course it seems empty, but, Good Lord! what's an artist made for except to transmute his pain into the world's beauty? You've got to *give*, man, you've got to give!"

"That's what *she* always said."

He slept next morning until nearly noon. But after breakfast at the *pâtisserie* around the corner he began to paint again. And every day after that he painted, no longer apprehensive of her coming in with a few sweet peas, or a book, or a pomegranate, saying, "It's your mouse, come to keep mouse-still," and presently, "But when you *are* through, darling ——"

"It's certainly true that the artist works best in pain," Gobby told him. He actually sounds envious, Elliott thought, squeezing the mounds of color onto his palette, screwing up his eyes to look at the waxy pears. "God! If you only knew!" he said under his breath.

Gobby was washing a pair of socks in Elliott's dishpan and did not at once answer. When he at last said, "Knew what?" Elliott was lost in trying to feel like a pear swelling juicily in a smooth yellow-pink skin, and only hummed a rising "Mmm?"

> "Alas, that Spring should vanish with the
>   Rose,
>   That Youth's sweet-scented manuscript
>   should close ——"

Christabel wrote in her Secret Journal, the day she read Elliott's brave farewell, and burned it. And for a long time her eyes filled with tears when she heard what they had called their tune, and had whistled to each other as a signal, although she never could be quite sure whether it was Nevin's "Narcissus" or "The Soldiers' Chorus" from "Faust."

Through veils of reticence she explained Elliott to Curtis, or tried to explain, for apparently he preferred to let Elliott remain a vague shadow.

"It wasn't love, dearest, not real love, like ours. It was compassion, I think. He seemed to *need* me so. It wasn't until you came that

I ever knew what love could be. I was like a prism, that's nothing—nothing, that is, except just a clearness and a pureness, I did keep *those*, I hope. And then the sun shines through the poor little prism and turns it into rainbow glory—and you're the sun! But he was only —— you're not listening to me, Curtis!"

"How can I listen to you when I'm looking at you? Do you know that you're the most beautiful girl in the world?"

"Darling! How strong you are!"

"How soon will you marry me? There's nothing to wait for."

And there wasn't. Aunt Deborah was well again and had offered Shady Lawn for the reception. Germantown was foaming with bloom and ready for the wedding. Bishop Lacombe would be off to Bar Harbor if they didn't hurry. Both families were delighted with the engagement. Christabel and Curtis would be in Paris on their wedding trip, so it would be foolish to spend much time on her trousseau. And, after all, when a great love comes, why wait?

For this is love, Christabel thought, as she lay awake after the day she had been with Curtis to choose her engagement ring. On the darkness, as vividly as if they had been drawn with a sharp pencil and painted with clear water-colors, she saw details that she had not consciously noticed. The sweep of Panama-hat brim, the black hat-band, the black silk tie with silver-gray dots, and a tuck-in of shadow under the knot, the scarlet carnation. She had read somewhere that intense emotion gives clairvoyance, that, when exaltation passes, memory of some detail remains forever as a sign. I never even noticed that he was wearing a carnation, she thought. Yet there it was, printed on the darkness, frilled and pinked as a penwiper. This is real love, she thought, touching the enormous sapphire. But she couldn't see his face. There was the expensive hat, the beautifully fitting soft collar, the tie, the carnation—and between them nothing, in spite of all her efforts.

The day drew near. In Mrs. Caine's bedroom Miss Plympton knelt to fit Christabel's wedding-gown.

"It's all wrong—everything's wrong! Look at this line! Just look at it! The whole idea was simplicity, not these dis*gust*ing little puckers and fullnesses!"

"I'm sorry, Miss Christabel. It was the way it was pinned up, and I thought we decided that was the way we wanted it."

"Don't work yourself up, darling. You're overtired."

Yes, she was tired. She shut her eyes and pressed her fingers to her temples.

"It will be all right."

"Mother, what *is* the use of saying it will be all right when it's all wrong?"

"If you could just hold still while I rip out the gathers, Miss Christabel, then we could drape it just the way you want."

Christabel gave a loud, exasperated sigh,

stood on one foot, stood on the other, put her hands to her head again.

"Sit down and rest a minute. You're worn out."

"While she's resting I'll run down and get the little nighties. They're just awfully dainty. I think you're going to love them!"

Christabel turned to Mrs. Caine as Miss Plympton scuttled from the room. "Well, mother, you see what a mess she's made of everything! I *told* you it was a mistake to have her."

"But, darling! She's made your clothes ever since your first little gingham dresses. It would have broken her heart to have anyone else make her Miss Christabel's wedding-dress. Besides, *I* think it looks all right, dear. And she needs the money dreadfully just now, with her mother breaking her ankle."

"Well, I'm *sorry*, but *really*! If you're seventy you oughtn't to climb trees."

"Darling, she just stood on a step-ladder to get some cherries for a pie ———"

94

"Well, it isn't *my* fault, and you act exactly as if it was—yes, you *do*, mother! And you know Miss Plympton absolutely *revels* in being a martyr. I wish I'd eloped, the way Curtis begged me to! Trousseau! What do I care for a trousseau? I'm just doing it to please you and the aunts."

"Darling——"

"I've explained to Miss Plympton till I'm hoarse that what I want this dress to look like is a novice's robes—oh, that reminds me! Mother!"

"Yes, dearie?"

"What did Mr. Leach say when you telephoned about that choir-boy?"

"I—I'll just slip down and call him up this minute."

"*Moth*er! Oh, I'm so sick of everybody promising to do things, and then *noth*ing gets done unless I attend to it."

"I'll call him up this minute, darling. I tried to get him this morning, but the line was busy, and then I had to see the florist——"

95

Left alone, Christabel lit a cigarette and sat smoking and frowning angrily, tapping a foot. Oh, she was tired! Her nerves were a nest of twittering sparrows. And everyone was being so stupid. This time, that should have been hushed, holy, tremulous with exquisite apprehension, was vulgarized by a stupid dressmaker getting things wrong, by the boy who sang the solos at Saint Mark's getting measles, by everyone being stupid and inconsiderate.

"Here's the nighties, dear!" Miss Plympton's eyes were swollen, her nose was pink and glazed. She had evidently taken the opportunity to have a cry. "Look — all eight of them. Mamma couldn't sleep last night, her ankle pained so, and I was sitting up, anyways, so I got them finished. Aren't they dainty?"

Christabel looked at one of the cobweb nightgowns, sighed, folded her lips.

"Isn't it all right, dear?"

"We don't seem to be having much luck, do we, Miss Plympton? I said ribbons under the net, and no lace. I gave you the lace to put on the camisoles. Have you put it on *all* of the nightgowns?"

Miss Plympton's eyes swam, her nose glowed.

"Well, we can't do anything about it now." Christabel sighed again. "Never mind. But please let's try to get this dress right."

Miss Plympton sank on her knees and began pulling with shaking hands at the satin folds. Christabel looked at herself in the mirror. The effect really was exquisite, after all. What a contrast the two reflected figures were. Her young loveliness glowing out of satin pure as snow in moonlight, Miss Plympton with her mouth full of pins, her red nose, her spectacles. Christabel's eyes grew softer as she looked from her own white beauty to the dumpy figure kneeling beside her. Poor old maid, spending her life sewing other women's wedding-dresses! It would make a poignant poem. She said, gently:

"There, that's lovely, Miss Plympton. I knew *you* could fix it."

Miss Plympton blew her nose violently. Christabel suddenly put her hands—how white they looked—on either side of the red face, and, tilting it up, bent to kiss it.

"There! And you mustn't mind what I said. It wasn't I who was talking; it was my tiredness and nervousness."

How simple an understanding heart makes everything, she thought, feeling bathed in Miss Plympton's love. How wonderful if we could all go to each other, and say simply, I'm sorry. But it takes love and courage. I was right about the pure white for the satin, she thought, gazing into the mirror. Not cream, like Ernestine's wedding-dress, that had turned her into a gigantic charlotte russe, but just this purity —a Madonna in alabaster. Of course not everyone can stand pure white.

In the mirror she saw her mother, and cried: "Look, mummy dear! Isn't it lovely now?"

"*Lovely*!" Mrs. Caine echoed. "Simply perfect! Mr. Leach says everything's all right, honey. He's gotten a boy from Saint Clem-

98

ent's for the solo. And a lot of new boxes have come. I told Jake to open them on the back porch. Curtis and Uncle Johnnie are looking at the presents."

"Uncle *John*nie! What's Uncle *John*nie doing here? There, that'll have to do, Miss Plympton."

"Wouldn't you like it just a crumb easier in the armholes?" asked Miss Plympton through pins, but Christabel was already struggling out of the satin folds.

She hurried into a dress and downstairs. From the landing window she caught a glimpse of Uncle Johnnie trotting to the gate, looking pleased with himself. Now what had he been saying, or not saying? She put the question to Curtis, wandering among clocks and dessert plates and cases of silver.

"What did you two find to talk about, dearest?"

"Why, I don't know exactly. Lots of things."

"Are you *dead?* Poor Curtis! Uncle John-

99

nie's a darling, of course, but he *is* old, and so he has ideas ———"

"I didn't notice that he had any. He seemed perfectly sensible to me."

"Did he? Do you know you're a very kind person? Oh, Curtis, it's a comfort to be with you! I'm ex*hausted! Things!*" She touched the gold soup plates from a family of Carey cousins with sad scornfulness. "Let's promise each other never to become the slaves of *things*, material possessions, Curtis."

"All right, let's. I thought that was awfully nice, that part you showed me in your Journal, where you wrote about wedding presents, and how you'd rather be given the moon than a silver tray. That reminds me, I know if you don't like the tray, Cousin Bessie would much rather have you exchange it for something you do like."

"Dearest, I a*dore* the tray! I only used it as a symbol. Don't you remember the other things I said, too—that I'd rather be given wild

100

raspberries than rubies, and a snowy branch of pine than an ermine cloak?"

"I'm going to get you an ermine cloak, all the same, or a sable one, if you'd rather."

"Oh, darling, *real*ly? Oh, you're so wonderful to me! How can I show you how much I love you?"

"By not getting all tired out. There's too much for you to do all the time. You must learn to let other people do things for you. I had no idea a wedding meant so much hullabaloo."

"And all so empty. I mean, what does anything matter except that you are mine and I am yours? These tribal laws, these sacrifices to tradition—they're all wrong. What do we care for laws, except the law of love? You know, Curtis, that what I would rather do would be simply to come home with you, across the fields, some evening when the frogs are piping and the west is pink, just you and I. You *do* know that, my lover, don't you?"

"I know, and I think it's wonderful of you,

darling, but still I guess we'd better go ahead and have some sort of ceremony. I mean, I was thinking about your mother and my mother. I suppose it would sort of worry them if we didn't. But I certainly am with you about thinking the simpler the better."

"Oh, *so* much better, dearest! If I considered myself—but, after all, does it matter so very much? If it's going to make the aunts and the dear little mothers happier to have the bishop and the choir-boys and lilies and organ thunder and all the old enchantments, does it matter so much what *we* want?"

"I don't believe you ever think of yourself."

"Oh, don't I! Don't I think about myself, and know I'm the happiest girl in the world? So happy that I feel wings fluttering—look and see if I haven't a pair of soap-bubble-colored wings!"

"I guess if you have wings they're angel wings."

"Darling! Not now! Some one's coming. Oh, Miss Plympton! Going home? You've met Mr. Carey, haven't you? Curtis, this is our dear Miss Plympton, whom we couldn't live without. She gave us that lovely pickle-fork, you remember. Wait, Miss Plympton. Will you take these to your mother, with my love?" She took an armful of roses from a vase and thrust them dripping into Miss Plympton's summer-silk arms, against her summer-silk bosom. "And tell her she must hurry up and get well for my wedding, because I refuse to have it without her."

Miss Plympton's eyes filled with tears again. "I'm sorry I was so stupid," she whispered. "I've got the—you-knows—with me. I can change that lace all right."

"Goo-*sie!* You're not to *touch* them if it's the least *bit* of trouble." Christabel dropped a kiss lightly on the crumpled cheek.

"I think she's—an angel," said Miss Plympton to Curtis, with a sniff, and he answered:

"That makes it unanimous, Miss Plympton."

Chapter Eight

UNCLE JOHNNIE followed Aunt Deborah up the aisle and into the front pew. Now, Deborah, hold your forehead with your fingertips as if it were beginning to ache, and I'll look into my hat.

He glanced sideways to see when she would lift her head. Almost nothing there but a smell of age, *eau de Cologne*, and new kid gloves, wrapped in a black silk mantle and topped by a bonnet, trembling so that the bonnet's glass dangles made a tiny clashing. Poor Deborah, you're getting very old.

Up we come! Ann and Susannah were in the front pew, too, and behind were the younger girls, Eliza, Lydia and Hannah. And here was Amy, weeping and delighted. She knew, for all her tears, that her daughter was doing well for herself. The Carey family across the aisle made an impressive showing.

Here came the bishop, fresh and rosy as a

104

baby just out of its bath, his starched sleeves two white billows against the white billows of marguerites on the altar, and Dr. Marsh, well laundered, too, looking as if he were going to give some one a nice but solemn surprise. They moved into sunlight falling through stained glass, and were wrapped in celestial crazy quilts of colored light.

The bridegroom and best man.

> "The *voice* that *breathed* o'er *E-ee-dun*,
>   That *earl*-yust wedding *day*,
> The *pri*mul marridge ble-uh-sing
>   It hahth not *pahssed* away."

The choir was rocking slowly by, splitting, filing into choir stalls.

> "Still *in* the *pure* es*pow*-ow-sul
>   Of *Chris*-chun mahn and *maid* ——"

Will she have her head down-drooping like a flower, Uncle Johnnie wondered, or bravely uplifted?

Bravely uplifted. Going into battle with all flags flying.

"What, Deborah?"

"I said, the blesséd child!"

Two little pages in green velvet carried her train. Curtis should have been in doublet and hose. He was the only one who looked out of place. Nice of her to let him come. Or did she know he was there? She seemed completely detached.

They were moving toward the altar now. Kneeling. Green and purple flakes of glory slid over the bishop's bald head and flowed down the bride's veil and train. She'd like that, Uncle Johnnie thought.

> "Oh, puffeck Love, all yuman thought
> trahnscending,"

a very young choir-boy sang, with his eyes rolled up. Which would win in a Looking Holy contest, he or Christabel? Uncle Johnnie wondered.

"——— that ye may so live together in this life, that in the world to come ye may have life everlasting." The bishop's words were

thick bubbles of honey. "Amen," the choir
sang seven times.

For a while Uncle Johnnie let ladies tell
him that it was a beautiful day, a beautiful
wedding, that Christabel was a beautiful bride,
that Shady Lawn was looking beautiful. Then,
understanding the feelings of one of the little
moss-green pages who was being sick behind a
mock-orange bush, he went to a rustic summerhouse, out of the way of the crowd. It was oc-
cupied by a young man in a large soft collar,
almost a fichu, Uncle Johnnie thought, eating
lobster salad.

"I hope I'm not intruding."

The young man's mouth was too full for
speech, but he made welcoming gestures with a
fork held by a hand whose wrist was encircled
by a silver-and-turquoise bangle, and Uncle
Johnnie sat down and yawned. The other
gave a final gulp.

"I couldn't stand watching them turn a sacrifice into a festival any more, so I came off
here by myself. My God! This is the kind of

107

thing that makes a man want to get dead drunk!"

"We could make a start," said Uncle Johnnie as a waiter passed by the summerhouse with a tray full of glasses of punch. "No, I don't want any of that vegetable soup. Go and get a bottle of champagne and two glasses."

"You couldn't stand it, either?"

"No, I couldn't."

"What's she doing it for, that's what I want to know? That exquisite girl throwing herself away."

"What's the matter with the groom, aside from his getting married?"

"Well, he's so evidently just a typical business man."

"Good family, rich."

"That would mean less than nothing to Christabel."

"Ah?"

The waiter's black face appeared in the doorway, framed in dangling sprays of roses. "Yas-

suh, yassuh, heah you ah, suh, all right suh?
Thank *you* suh, thank you kindly suh!" The
gentlemen buried their noses in spray.

"She's as near pure spirit as anyone I ever
knew. Why, Christabel is almost a religion
to the people who really know her."

"Indeed!"

"What *is* she doing this for? Did you notice her expression? White as death, and those
shining eyes—there was a sort of tragic radiance about her. You know she looked more
like a nun than a bride, the way she wore her
veil like a wimple, and carried that one Madonna lily. All the time I kept feeling that
what was really happening was that she was
taking the veil. I kept thinking, what is that
man doing there?"

"That was rather the effect. Let me fill your
glass."

"Thank you. *Salut!* The sunlight coming
through the leaves turns your face a very interesting green, sir. I should like to paint it."

"Ah, you're a painter?"

"Well, yes, although my work isn't what the Philistine means when he says painting. In fact, I don't confine myself to paint. I use any medium that I feel will express my meaning most truly. And the thing I try to do is, I try to escape from convention into pure abstraction. I'm not interested in your mustache, for instance, or your nose, but in your essential personality. But I don't want to talk about myself."

"Not at all."

"I feel that convention means death to art, emotion, spirit. Thank you. *Salut! Shoo!* How these roses attract the bees! Speaking of convention, don't you agree with me that it's wonderful for a girl like Christabel to have escaped so completely from the death in life of the conventions she was brought up in?"

"You feel that?"

"Oh, absolutely." He flapped a hand at a bee. "You know there's no one in her family who understands her—love, yes, she must be given that wherever she goes, I think, but un-

110

derstanding, no! It almost killed her to get away from them. She used to tell us about it. Very sweetly and understandingly, but you could tell what she'd been through. And now that I've seen it all for myself, I can realize what a hell her life here must have been to her."

"As bad as all that? . . . I don't think that kind stings."

"Don't you? It looks terribly angry. Just watch it worrying that rose! What were we saying? Oh, Christabel! Well, just look around you, sir! Just feel the atmosphere. But she did get out into the light and air, and yet now of her own free will she's going back into darkness like—like—Persephone, and nobody's stopping her. When I looked at the priests and the flowers, and Christabel with her white face, I could think of just one word. Sacrifice."

I thought of that word, too, Uncle Johnnie said to himself. There was also the bridegroom's red face. Red as a rose was he. I shall have to lend this young man my handkerchief in a minute.

"Maybe she can take care of herself," he added aloud.

"I know her as perhaps you don't, sir."

"I think that's highly probable."

They finished the champagne in a silence broken by the roaring of the bees, and presently by distant shouts.

"They must be going away."

The victoria was at the door, with Deborah's new coachman, beaming red face and big white wedding-favor. "So pretty and touching to see how the old family servants adore her!" Uncle Johnnie heard a strange lady say reverently.

Around the front steps people were calling, laughing, their hands full of rice. But when Christabel came slowly out, more nunlike than ever in pale gray, her face whitely, stilly shining, hands fell, rice dribbled to the ground.

"Good-by, good-by! Good-by, Gobby dear. Good-by, dear Uncle Johnnie."

If I'd let out a cloud of sulphur and switched a tail at him he couldn't have been more scared, thought Uncle Johnnie, looking at the place from which the young man had vanished.

Chapter Nine

"WOULD you like to play bridge with the Prestons, Christabel?"

"Curtis *dar*ling! Play *bridge*, with the sea and the sky looking like this?"

"Well, what would you like to do?"

"Dearest, must we *do* something all the time? Can't we just *be?*"

So for a few minutes they just were. How blue the sea is! she thought. How utterly it satisfies me! She looked toward Curtis to see if he were drinking it in, too. His eyes were shut, his mouth a little open.

Why was I such a fool as to think there could never be anything for me but loneliness? What is life, anyway, but just being alone, never really touching each other, except in those rare moments when a shared beauty, a shared reality, opens the prison doors? How I long to share with him this rapture of really seeing the blue of sea and sky. And here he is, beside me—asleep.

It seemed almost a symbol.

How Elliott would have gloried in this light, this benediction of color.

I am utterly lonely, I might as well admit it, she thought, tears stinging into her eyes. In this shipful of people I am all alone.

Of course they made a fuss about her. People always did, over anyone who was well known. And although she had begged Curtis not to tell anyone she was Christabel Caine, he was so proud of her he couldn't resist bragging, and he had given away a dozen copies of *Carnation Flower* already. He must have brought half a trunkful. It was a little ridiculous, like a drummer giving away free samples. There was something about Curtis—not an insensitiveness, exactly ——

She smiled at the Misses White, trotting past, with their arms full of bags, cushions, *Cathedral Towns of England*, *Châteaux of Old France*, *My Trip Abroad*, and a bristle of knitting-needles and fountain pens. Poor little old maids, so excited at meeting a writer. Poor little trippers, brave little Christopher Columbuses! She must ask them to tea in London, if she had time. They would be thrilled.

Louis Brown strolled by, lifting his eyebrows and thrusting out his lower lip as he looked from sleeping Curtis to her, and she smiled, lifted her eyebrows, too, drifted her hands through the air. A feeling of being understood warmed her heart. But I must keep him from caring too much, she thought. He mustn't be hurt—and neither must my Curtis. She turned her eyes, that had followed Louis along the deck, to her husband.

He really did look silly. She dropped a book with a bang, and he struggled up with a yawn that was almost a scream.

"Why don't *you* go and get into a bridge game, Curtis?"

"Well, I don't like to leave you."

"I want to be alone with the sea. I want to

116

look at it until there isn't any me left, until there isn't anything left but blueness."

"*Sure* you won't be lonely?"

She smiled at him, and kissed her finger tips. He is just a grown-up little boy, eager to get to his toys. My grown-up little boy, who adores me so that it almost breaks my heart. When he turned to look back at her from the smoke-room door she smiled again, but she saw him through tears that splintered the world into crystals.

Loneliness ———

Courage, child. Wrap the sky around you, comfort yourself with the sea.

Perhaps Louis would be coming back.

But the deck remained deserted, and the dazzle of sun on water made her blink. Getting up to pull her chair around, she could look into a smoke-room window. The interior, its darkness swimming with scarlet balls to her sun-dazzled eyes, slowly revealed Curtis with his back to her, awake and lively enough now, with the Prestons, and Mrs. Sloane, who chose that moment to answer some remark of his with a friendly shove and shout of laughter.

Why did he marry me? Christabel asked herself, sinking into her chair. If that's what he wants, why did he take me away from the people I love, the people who love me? Suppose I should go overboard, how much would he really care? He would be sorry, of course, and wear correct mourning, and give a stained glass window to the church where we were married—Christabel, dearly beloved wife of Curtis Carey—and then he would play bridge with Mrs. Sloane.

The current volume of her Secret Journal lay on the deck by her chair. She picked it up and began to write.

"What peace it would be to say, I am too tired to go on. To let my body enter the sea, and sink, down, down, past goggling fish with drifting films of tail, past ribbons of ruffled sea-weed, purple and brown ———"

People were coming out from their afternoon naps. With her eyes on the words that

118

streamed from her pen she felt them going by, felt them looking at her. "—writing—" she heard them murmur to each other respectfully. "—writing." They think I have more than my share, she told herself. They think I am young, beautiful, rich, brilliant, beloved— happy. They envy me.

If they only knew!

"To sink slowly, slowly, down to the trees of white and rose-red coral massed with bubbles, to the sprays of pearl, to drift and turn until my bones were white and delicate, covered with small rose-pink shells and silver bubbles, drifting and turning forever in that still depth of peace."

A group of skirts and trousers surrounded her chair. People! When all she wanted was to be alone. "Peace ——" she wrote again, and rose from the depths of the sea.

"Pardon us for interrupting ——"

"What is *prob*ably a masterpiece in the making!"

"We've come to ask a very, very great favor."

She felt her eyes and mouth as round as an astonished child's, she touched her bosom delicately with outspread fingers.

"A favor? Of *me?*"

"We've been chosen as a committee to beg, bribe, or otherwise cajole you into giving a reading from your poems for the edification and delight of your fellow passengers."

"Please say you will!"

"Everyone wants to hear you!"

"We won't take no for an answer."

"Oh, *thank* you for wanting me to—but I can't! No, I can't!"

"Oh, *please!*"

"I tremble to think of the fate of the committee if it ventures to withdraw without your promise."

"Oh, but if you only knew how it *terr*ifies me! No, no, I really can't!"

"Just *think* of the pleasure you'll be giving."

120

"You can't refuse when everyone wants so *much* to hear you."

"May I put in a special plea for 'Out where the long sea road Follows the curve of the cliff'?"

"Oh yes, *ex*quisite!"

"And please, please, pretty-please, some of those darling kiddie poems!"

Tender assenting groans.

No longer the lonely cold depths of the sea. She rocked gently in the warm sun. They were being too kind, she told them, they were making too much of a fuss over her little songs. She thanked them for it, she loved them for it—but, no.

"Don't say that. Think it over and tell us this evening."

I can't do it, she thought, going down the stateroom. To get up and read in front of all those people! They don't realize how a thing like that *drains* you, if you're sensitive enough to have written the poems in the first place.

Yet if I have been given something precious,

have I any right not to share it? Isn't this sacrifice of pouring forth, part of my gift and my
burden? She opened the closet door and
looked absently at her dresses.

If she did read to them, what poems would
she choose?

> White lilac, delicate and cool,
> And purple lilac, dark with rain——

She tried it softly, watching herself in the long
mirror. And as she spoke she became a lilac
bush, delicate and cool. Elliott had said once
that he must feel like what he was painting,
and ever since then she had realized that she,
too, must be what she created—she must be
lilac, the sea wind crying, falling rain. She
must be everything.

She was in his studio again, curled up in the
window seat, hearing his words. She saw his
old painting-shirt open at the throat, the fringe
of hair she loved to run her finger under, vermilion spikes on table and canvas, for he had
been feeling like red-hot pokers when he spoke.

"Dear Elliott!" she whispered, leaning against the closet door. Then she caught her breath, flung her head back bravely. Courage, child ——

There hung a golden gown she had never worn. It reminded her of something Louis Brown had said last night. "I'm the only one who's on to you. Everyone else thinks you're a little golden queen, but I know you're just a ridiculous beautiful child who has learned, God knows how, to cast a spell."

Smiling, she slipped into the gown. She put on her pearls, patted a film of powder over her face, and interestedly did a little work with her eyebrow pencil. Her white face and shadowed eyes made her feel frail and exquisite. She moved her white hands against her golden gown.

> White lilac, delicate and cool,
> And purple lilac, dark with rain ——

She heard Curtis talking to the steward, and had just time to scramble out of her dress before he came in.

123

She threw her arms around him, she loved him and silently forgave him.

"Well, what's new?"

If only he wouldn't always greet her that way!

"Nothing—oh, they want me to give a reading of my poems."

"Fine!"

"*Fine?* I don't know what you mean. I hate the idea. Anything like that leaves me utterly *spent*."

"Oh, you'll enjoy it."

She felt ready to burst. We are utter strangers, she thought, as they dressed for dinner, getting into each other's way. He thinks I *like* getting up and having everybody look at me, when it kills me—when I can only bear it because I have something real, something true, something of myself to give them. It was a good thing she hadn't worn the golden gown before. A little golden queen. She heard herself speaking exquisite words, she saw Louis Brown's dark face in the audience. White

124

lilac, delicate and cool. And running along with her thoughts was Curtis's voice, telling her what bad hands he had held, and what nice women Mrs. Preston and Zita Sloane were.

He had gone to get cigarettes after dinner, when Louis Brown carried her off to look at the stars. Standing by the rail, she felt the music from the distant orchestra, the long rays of light, her own voice, exquisite and sad, trailing out from the ship, delicate tendrils that found only darkness to cling to. All up her arm she felt how Louis wanted to cover her hand, lying white on the rail, with his.

And this moment of ours—this moment— already is the past.

She could hear him breathing hard through his nose. It was time she said something.

"Sometimes I think I'd like to go over the side of the ship, and just sink down into peace. Think of what you'd go drifting through—red and white coral trees all covered with silver bubbles, and ruffled ribbons of seaweed, and the ocean to rock you to sleep. Wouldn't you like to drift in the dim green light forever, with no more restlessness?"

He continued to breathe hard through his nose.

"Wouldn't you, Louis?"

"I haven't been listening to you. How can I hear you when I'm looking at you?"

Oh, my poor dear, you mustn't love me so, she thought. She put one cool finger tip against his lips.

"Ironical, our meeting on your wedding trip, isn't it?" he asked. And although he had recovered his usual tone of light bitterness, she felt his love pouring over her. It made her love Curtis, who at that moment joined them, made her greet him radiantly, tenderly, putting her hand through his arm, her eyes on Louis.

All through dinner Christabel's voice had come to Curtis from far away, her eyes had been a wounded deer's, and afterward she had disappeared. He had been looking for her all evening. Somehow he must make up to her

126

for having hurt her, though what he had done he didn't know. She was so sensitive, so tender-hearted, that he was always putting his foot in it, when he only wanted to make her happy. Perhaps it's just the artistic temperament, he thought.

This afternoon he had had a struggle to keep awake. Two cocktails before lunch, a bottle of stout, and the sun on the waves had caused an agonizing struggle, followed by oblivion, but something had made him sit up with a jerk, had made the rail, the life-preserver, his own cocked-up feet swim back into their places, before Christabel noticed that he had dozed off, he was almost sure. So she couldn't have been hurt by that, or by his playing bridge, for she had suggested it.

It had been a good game. He thought of Zita, and how she had laughed at his jokes and looked at him as he lit her cigarette. He seemed to be able to please some women. He didn't know what was the matter with Christabel.

He found her with Mr. Brown, he insolently

close, as usual. Christabel drew away from him
and put her arm through Curtis's, saying that
Mr. Brown was showing her the stars. That
is Ursa Major, said Mr. Brown, and Curtis
said, the only constellation he could recognize
was the good old Dipper. And Christabel
said the floor of heaven was thick inlaid with
patines of bright gold. A respectful silence
followed this, and then Mr. Brown said he
would hope to see them later, and left.

"Well! I've been looking all over the ship
for you!" said Curtis.

"Darling, you mustn't be jealous."

"Jealous! Of *that?*"

She rubbed her cheek against his sleeve.
"Ooh, I'm so glad you've come! You've left
me pretty much alone today." She lifted his
hand and left a kiss in the palm. She's forgiving me, he thought, with mixed relief and
indignation, for he had meant to forgive her.

"I don't know what's been the matter,
Christabel. •I knew I was in Dutch some way."

"Ridiculous boy!"

128

"It wasn't because I played bridge, was it?"

She was silent. It was, he thought, and said aloud:

"But, Christabel, you said ——"

"Said? *Said?* Curtis, don't you know there's a language deeper than words, that the heart understands?"

"But I ——"

"I wasn't going to tell you. I wasn't going *ever* to let you know!"

"But ——"

"But, oh, *Cur*tis, you hurt me so this afternoon! I was so lonely I wanted to die!"

"But you said ——"

"I didn't want you to stay with me if you wanted to be with them. If you would rather be with Mrs. Preston and that Mrs. Sloane, I *want* you to be with them."

"But I *asked* you ——"

"Only don't expect *me* to come, too, because they make a spiritual atmosphere that I simply can't—*breathe* in."

"Oh, now, what's the matter with them?"

"So ma*t*erial—so self-centered."

"But Zita Sloane's nice-looking and polite
____"

"Curtis, she's just *cheap*. Bracelets like a Fiji Islander, and powder enough on her nose to make an avalanche. I don't care for *myself*, but I'm so ashamed for *you*, to see you taken in by a type like that."

She's really jealous, he thought, in a pleased glow. She loves me even more than I realized. "I can't remember what she looks like," he said. "When I look at you I can't remember what anyone else looks like."

She drew close to him again.

"And this evening I waited for you and I *waited* for you, and you didn't come! I didn't want to be sharing this starlight with *him*. I wanted you!"

"But, my darling, I was hunting for you everywhere." And he thought, I must never leave her unless I absolutely have to.

"I wanted you so!"

How she loves me, he thought, lifting her fingers to kiss.

"Isn't it beautiful, sailing into the night? It's like coming home again, home into the heart of God."

"It certainly is."

That was inadequate. He felt unworthy of his wonderful girl, who had given herself to him so completely. And as they stood in silence he was ashamed of himself for suddenly thinking how much he would like a whisky and soda and a cheese sandwich. He managed to get his wrist watch into the light without her noticing. Almost smoke-room closing time. But somehow he couldn't mention it to Christabel.

Her face was lifted to the stars, a long end of the white veil she had bound around her silky head molded itself to his features.

"We're very close at times like this, aren't we, my husband?"

Chapter Ten

LADY DICKERY's motor car, with a coronet on the door and a footman beside the chauffeur, purred toward Knightsbridge, taking Christabel and Curtis to their hotel, from the dinner Lady Dickery had given in their honor.

"It's just like Caroline not to let us take a taxi," Curtis said. "She never can do enough for people. Even when she was a little girl she was always giving away everything. She took off some coral beads Aunt Ethel gave her, I remember once, and gave them to a little darky; they couldn't stop her. They never could make her mind, Ma'm'selle or Fräulein or any of them. I remember her sailing a new hat in a muddy brook, and she used to buy balloons just to sit on and pop, and hide under the table in her nightgown when Aunt Ethel was giving a dinner. The homeliest little mug, with spectacles and big front teeth, and language—boy! But everyone was crazy about her, just the way they are now. Well, you can see for yourself why they would be, she's always been so warm-hearted and generous."

Yes, so generous! Christabel thought, drawing away from him into her corner. All she wants is to give, give, give, to be the source of blessings, like God! Giving, and letting everybody know she's giving. Grabbing the center of the stage all evening!

"Don't you think she's nice?"

There was a little silence before Christabel answered, "Very nice." And after another silence, "But ——"

"But what?"

"Oh, nothing. Only it's strange, isn't it, that all these years in England haven't made her voice gentler?" She listened to her own voice, that sounded even more gentle and musical than usual, as she remembered hearing through the noise of the big dinner party how Caroline screamed at the sight of herself in a Watteau shepherdess hat, how Dickery was eating nothing but pineapples because of his fat stomach.

133

"Oh, well, she always did speak out. She wants us to come down to Clouds next week—did she ask you? You'll be crazy about it. There's a moat and a ghost and a secret passage, and gardens enough even for you. I told her what a gardener you were, and she's crazy to show you the gardens. There's some famous old clipped yew, too—I don't know much about it, but it's in all the books. And they're sure to have interesting people. I think it would be fun. Don't you?"

"Of course we'll go if you want to, Curtis."

"But don't *you* want to? You'd enjoy it, Christabel."

"I suppose I could look at the clipped yew while the *in*teresting people amused each other."

"Why ——?"

"I've never in my life been treated the way I was tonight, Curtis! I wouldn't treat a *crim*inal the way I was treated!"

"Why, I ——!"

"I suppose it's fashionable not to introduce

people and talk across them about things they can't possibly understand. Well, if it is, I don't want to be fashionable! I *hate* people who are so self-centered and conceited!"

"Why, darling! I thought you were having such a good time!"

She bit her lip and turned her head away.

"I thought you'd be crazy about Caroline! And she wants to do so much for us. She wants us to come to her later for the hunting. Wait till you see the way that woman rides! Gosh! I'd love to get some hunting!"

"The cruelty—little bright-eyed furry creatures—it's sickening!" Christabel shuddered, pulling her ermine wrap closer about her.

There was another silence before Curtis's anxious voice asked, "Is your head worse, darling?"

"My head?" she almost questioned, before she remembered that was the reason she had given for not going on to a dance with the others, as Curtis wanted to. She sighed, turned to him with a brave little smile, let a snowflake

135

hand fall into his. But in their room, when Curtis began again about how he would like to go to Clouds, she burst into tears.

"Why, Christabel ——!"

She could have stopped, but she made herself go on, remembering shell-pink Lady Somebody or other, pointed out to her by Lord Dickery as the most beautiful woman in London, pug-nosed Princess de Something, who had everybody laughing. And that fat old duchess with her patronizing inflections, saying, when Christabel had finally made her understand that she was a writer: "Oh, indeed! A very pleasant hobby, no doubt." Above all, hideous loud-voiced Caroline, showing-off, dominating. I *hate* her, Christabel thought, not able now to stop her sobs. Oh, I'm so homesick, so homesick! They love me at home; they understand me. I want my own darling mother ——

She grew quieter at last, drinking the water that Curtis brought, and then lying exhausted in his arms. Her heart ached for herself, so sensitive and fragile.

136

"Darling, we won't go to Clouds. We won't do anything you don't want to do."

"We *will* go to Clouds! You must, to show you've forgiven me for being so silly—darling, dearest Curtis!" She pressed her tear-wet cheek against his as his arms tightened around her.

When she woke next morning Curtis had gone out. Her maid drew her bath and ordered her breakfast. A haystack of flowers had come from Caroline Dickery, with a note hoping that her head was better. Christabel made a face as she read it, and tore it into bits. On one bit a coronet was left intact, and she put it into her book as a marker. How childish the British were, with all their little symbols of this and that, dressing up and saying, now I am important. She pulled the paper out so the coronet showed, and looked thoughtfully at pearls and strawberry leaves.

"Ring for some vases, Minnie," she said. And when the hotel maid was bringing them in, and Minnie was shaking out the dewy tangle, she added: "They're so lovely and fresh, I suppose Lady Dickery has them sent up from her country place."

The hotel maid looked impressed by Lady Dickery's name. Amusing! Christabel thought. The English certainly are snobs.

She enjoyed a peach with a fluff of cotton wool still clinging to it, eggs, bacon, toast and jam, and although the coffee wasn't much, she managed three cups. Then she lay among her pillows, watching the lace slide back from her white lifted arms. She could see herself in two mirrors, and see repeated trunks, two other Minnies in small pleated black aprons, masses of flowers foaming and spraying. And suddenly she thought, if only Elliott could see me now!

Minnie went out with the gown Christabel had worn last night a crystal waterfall over her arm. She saw herself as she must have looked in it, coming down the marble staircase; she heard again the footmen echoing her name. Of all the affected ways of living!

138

Again she thought of Elliott. He would have really seen her in that gown, like a water-nymph in drops of bright water. Curtis had never even mentioned it.

In her mind she began to compose a letter to Elliott. Perhaps it would open old wounds too cruelly. But if she wrote to Boyd, she could depend on Elliott's seeing it. She got her portfolio.

"Curtis's cousin, Lady Dickery, gave a simply *huge* dinner for us last night," she wrote. "The guests were really nothing compared with the grandeur of the footmen, about a million of them, all with powdered hair, but they did the best they could for people who were only Dukes and Duchesses and Prime Ministers and such. Caroline Dickery is the kind of person you generally see pictures of in *The Sketch* or *The Tatler*, with a pull-on hat and large capable feet and a terrier, labeled 'Lady Dickery and Friend,' but last night she had diamonds every place but the tip of her nose, and so had all the other women, tiaras and everything—and diplomats all done up with blue ribbons—*and*—little me the center of it all!

"It's like a Fairy Tale. And it's hard work I have to keep the chuckles back when I think of myself in my old smock dining on an apple and a bun, with the coffee-pot bubbling on the gas ring, and then catch a glimpse of this new Christabel dressed in crystal and cloth of silver, going in to dinner on a Noble Arm, and I wonder, when Midnight strikes, will Cinderella be back in her old smock and go running out through rows of 'stonished flunkies? And then Cinderella's heart gives a leap as she thinks— if she could! But she can't. Her Rolls-Royce doesn't change into a pumpkin when Midnight strikes, her crystal gown doesn't change into the old smock, and it's only her Heart can come Home.

"I don't mean that, Boyd dear. I'm a very happy Child. But—but—I do get homesick, I do miss my friends.

"Do you ever see Elliott? I think of him so often.

"Caroline wants us to come to Clouds (their wonderful old country seat) for a house party, but I'm awfully afraid my Curtis isn't going to let me go, as I haven't been very well (I'm writing this in bed, surrounded by flowers and notes and invitations—if my head isn't turned forever it won't be the fault of all these kind, kind people). There's nothing really the matter with me, but my big boy is so strong himself that he seems to think I'm a Delicate Child made of Spun Glass and Thistledown, and spoils me accordingly. He's a Sweet Person, and it isn't his fault that he doesn't love to go adventuring, the way we do, so that I've had to steal off by my own little lonely self to ———"

To do what? What were some of the things she was going to do as soon as she had a minute? Ride on a bus-top, have tea at an A. B. C. "—ride on a Bus, high up in the air over the Bobbies with their faces like scarlet peonies, and the costers' patient little gray donkeys, and have tea and Bath buns at an

A. B. C.—such fun! Only—I do want some one to Play With!"

That would tell them she was still their Christabel, simple and unspoiled. And really, she could hardly wait to do those things.

Curtis had left a note saying he would be back at twelve, and it was quarter to. She finished her letter, got up, and drew the curtains close together. She was lying in the dark when he opened the door cautiously, and lifted a drooping hand to greet him.

"How are you, darling?"

"I'm *all* right, dearest. Kiss me."

"You're not all right, or you wouldn't have the room dark. Couldn't you eat something if I ordered it? A little soup? Some grapes?"

She shook her head.

"I'm going to get a doctor."

"Curtis, my *dar*ling, I'm all right! Just— lazy."

"You're a little liar, that's what you are. You sound as weak as a drowned kitten."

She powdered her nose and put on her pearls

142

while Curtis was getting the doctor, a delightful man with spats and a monocle. She gave him one of Caroline's carnations for his buttonhole, and he agreed with her that she had better get out of London if she had felt ill and depressed ever since she arrived.

"Dear boy, you *must*n't worry so!" she told Curtis, smoothing the lines from his forehead with gentle finger tips. "It's just that London doesn't suit me."

"Well, how about going down to Caroline's? The country, and quiet, and everything?"

"I asked him, but he was awfully down on the idea, the excitement of a big party and all. I'm *so* apologetic! But *you* go, darling! I'll be all right! I'll just go quietly somewhere. You go without me! *Please!*"

"Where does he think you ought to go? Where would you like to?"

"I don't care. Anywhere—*any*where, so long as it's with you! Somewhere where it will be just us alone, darling."

So they went to Paris.

143

Chapter Eleven

I T WAS a Paris Christabel had not known
before, under the Tomb of Napoleon
Louvre Now Girls chaperonage of Edith Johnson Plummer. After London it seemed like
heaven, at first. It was enough just to have
salad mean brittle ice-green frills of lettuce and
dark needles of chopped chives instead of a stew
of tinned fruits; just to pour crystals of *Jasmin*,
Giroflée Jaune, *L'Heure Exquise*, into her
baths; to have hot golden *café au lait* and flaky
croissants instead of mud and water and cold
toast; to get into a taxi with her arms full of
packages and say "The Ritz." She brought
back packages, she had them sent, their rooms
rattled with tissue paper as Minnie unpacked
boxes. "When I was here before I bought a
chemise and nightie to match, and thought I
had Paris lingerie!" she told Curtis with
amused tenderness for the child she had been,
while the waiter tried to find room for their

breakfast tray among drifts of silk and chiffon, apricot, ivory, and mauve.

But after a while she grew restless. Perhaps we ought to see other people, she thought, looking through the *Herald* to see if she could find any names she knew. We mustn't let our happiness make us selfish.

And what was the use of all her new gowns if there was no one to show them to? Curtis never noticed what she had on, unless she called his attention to it, and even with her generous Curtis it was just as well not to call attention to too many all at once, for when you are a type that demands special creations, dresses are expensive. Their first misunderstanding had come when he had seen the bill for the seven picture gowns. And after he had said that he wanted to spend his whole life in making her happy! She had been so hurt that he had given her a sapphire bracelet next day. She twisted it on her wrist now. Dark blue fire on snow.

> "And blessings on the falling out
> That all the more endears—"

she said to herself, letting it slip up her arm, down over her hand. Then she lifted it to her lips, whispering: "And kissed again with tears!"

Curtis was out looking up a business connection, and she was bored and lonely. She didn't want to write, she didn't want to read, she didn't want to stay indoors, and yet she could think of nothing she wanted to go shopping for. Still, in Paris one could always buy gloves.

As she stepped out of the lift she saw Gobby Witherspoon.

"Gobby!"

"For *Heav*en's sake! Christabel!"

Darling Gobby! Dear, faithful, loving Gobby! She let her hands lie in his.

"How did you know I was here? And how did you know that this afternoon, of all afternoons, I needed you?"

"My subconscious must have gotten a message, because my conscious certainly thought you were still in London."

"And you felt me here so strongly that you

146

came to me! My dear, do you know that touches something very deep?"

They looked at each other deeply. And then her mood changed. She clapped her hands.

"Now can you play with me a little while, Gobby? I'm all alone this afternoon. Curtis had other things to do. Can't we just wander about like a couple of children on a holiday, and be utterly silly and happy?"

"I'd *love* to, but——"

"Perhaps you have an engagement?"

"Oh *no!* But—if you'll just excuse me one minute—I——"

"Certainly, Gobby."

"I—well, you see my garter broke, and I came in to fix it ——"

He really is a little absurd, she thought, waiting for him. Subconsciousness, indeed! Sometimes she couldn't help feeling that he wasn't as real a person as he might be, that he was inclined to pose. But her heart warmed to him again as he came back, rather pink, from fixing his garter.

"Let's go somewhere away from the shops, Gobby. I'm sick of them. How horrid of me to say that! When my Curtis has been so generous, so much too generous to me! But I'm so tired of being dressed up like a big doll—I want to be a woman, a breathing, feeling woman, not a beautiful doll that opens and shuts her eyes and wears pretty clothes."

"Aren't you happy, Christabel?"

"Oh yes, I suppose so. At least—is anyone happy? Oh, what's the use of not being honest with you, Gobby? You, being you, would know, no matter what I told you. I'm happy this afternoon, anyway! Look at those big fern-fringed willow baskets full of snails! Look at those apples with flowers and stars— what do they do, paste paper patterns on them before they're ripe? I'd rather have that pink-and-yellow apple with the pale green hearts on it than all the jewels in the Rue de la Paix."

"You *have*n't changed, thank God!"

"Haven't I, Gobby? I feel as if I had. I wouldn't say this to anyone in the world but

148

you, but I feel changed to the depths of my soul. But let's not talk about me; let's talk about you. Oh, Gobby dear, this is heaven! My big boy loves the restaurants that everybody goes to, and the theaters, places where you meet every American in Paris! And I *can't* let him know that I don't enjoy them. I put on my pretty new dresses, and I try to pretend I'm loving it all as much as he is. That's what a woman has to learn, through love and pity, to pretend she's happy doing whatever her man wants to do. But men don't pretend—they're like children that way, I think. Curtis is a sweet person, but he just couldn't understand the thrill of playing around like this, and why I love it so. Gobby! My *dear!* A street fair!"

"What shall I buy you? I want to buy you something."

"Buy me that gingerbread pig named René —no, no, this one named Louis—and I'll keep it forever to remember you by."

They looked at strong men and white mice,

and Gobby modestly averted his eyes from four respectable Parisians, two beards, two black silk dresses, squeezed into a giant *pot-de-chambre* on the merry-go-round, answering with shrill screams the light-hearted remarks of by-standing friends. Then, leaving the fair, they paused for refreshments outside a café.

"An *aperitif* for me, please."

"*Deux aperitifs—oh! non, un moment! Un aperitif pour madame et une tasse de chocolat pour moi.*"

"Thank you, sir. Any pastry?"

"*Oh, oui, patisserie assorti.* I'm crazy about that frock, Christabel, that little glimpse of lemon-yellow sash is heavenly with the green, but you *must*n't wear that hat with it, my dear! The color's all right, but the line isn't *you*. I'll have to take you to a wonderful place where they make hats on your head. Are you sure you aren't just being unselfish, leaving that coffee éclair for me?"

"It's being a wonderful afternoon, Gobby! It's giving me fresh courage to go on with."

"I wish you were happier."

"Is it so very important? And I *have* been happy this afternoon, thanks to you! But I don't want to talk about me—you're such an understanding person you lead me astray. Tell me about yourself. Have you seen Elliott since—I——?"

"I went to see him the day after your wedding. I wonder if I ought to tell you about it? Of course I don't have to ask *you* never to breathe a word to a soul."

"Of *course* not, Gobby!"

"Well, I thought he'd be pretty low—you know—so I hurried down from the train; I thought maybe I could sort of cheer him up or something, well, not exactly cheer him up, but, anyway, I went down, and of course I went in without knocking, as usual—*don't* ever tell!"

"Gobby, don't you *know* me?"

"Well, he was standing there with a face like death, and holding a blue bottle. I didn't stop to speak, even; I just ran at him and dashed it out of his hand and it smashed to the

151

floor. I saw a piece of the bottle; it had a skull and cross-bones on it!"

"Oh, Gobby! Oh, my poor, poor Elliott! Thank God you got there in time!"

"Of course I pretended it was an accident. I think I said I was trying to catch a moth or something, and that my foot slipped. And he was wonderful, Christabel, the way he pulled himself together. You'd have been proud of him. He got off some story about developing some photographs and having to have acids and things."

"Oh, what courage! What a gallant lie!"

"Of course he did have a lot of other bottles and powders and things there. He *might* have been telling the truth."

"Oh no, Gobby, you don't know Elliott if you think that. Don't you see, it was to make it seem natural? He knew I would blame myself, and he didn't want to hurt me. Oh, my poor, poor boy, what he must have suffered! I don't know whether this makes me feel most sad or most proud!"

"Well, then we wiped up the mess, and then I didn't like to leave him, so I got him to come to the Zoo with me. I was awfully glad I thought of it; it seemed to sort of take his mind off things. He was simply crazy about the blue-bottomed mandril. I was, too. Did you ever see it? I never saw such a combination of repulsiveness and beauty; it made my blood run cold. This huge baboon, with teeny little eyes, like a pig, and bright blue-and-red striped cheeks that look as if they'd been flayed, and the most horrible scarlet lips showing through a beard, like the world's worst nightmare of King Edward the Seventh, and then this *exquisite* behind—my dear, such colors!"

"Did Elliott ———?"

"Wait till I tell you—cerulean blue and deep rose and mauve, melting into each other. Elliott was crazy to paint him; in fact, he was just starting when I left New York."

"He *is* going on, then? Oh, the gallant gentleman!"

She pressed her hands together to stop their

trembling. Her body trembled with love and pity because Elliott had been ready to kill himself when she had married some one else, with pride because he had the courage to live so that she should not be hurt. How he must have loved her! More, even, than she had guessed. She put her hand to her throat, suddenly breathless. "What a beauty!" Gobby exclaimed, noticing her sapphire bracelet.

She came back from the real world of intense feeling to the dream world of the sapphire bracelet, Gobby, the stack of franc-marked saucers. Already the lamps were printing shadow plane-leaves on the sidewalk. She must go back to Curtis.

"You've saved my life, my dear," she told Gobby as he left her at the Ritz. "And since you've done so much for me, will you do one thing more? Will you forget everything I've said, and just remember, Christabel *is* happy?"

Chapter Twelve

"OH, LOVELY DAY! Oh, Day of Shining Hours!" Christabel wrote in her Secret Journal. "For this day My Man and I came home to

OUR HOUSE

And the sun shone, and the winds blew, and the very sparrows in the gutter put on a glory.

"Curtis carried me in over the doorstep, according to the old Gaelic custom of Bringing Home the Bride ——"

She paused, remembering how embarrassed Curtis had been, with Smedley opening the door, and Bates following with their bags. He had carried her in, as she suggested—he, dear boy, had never heard of the old custom—but his face had been scarlet. It had hurt her deeply that he could care, at such a time, for what servants might be thinking, but now she could smile as she sighed. That was the very fabric of a woman's love for a man—understanding, forgiveness, and always that hidden, half-sad laughter at the little boy who would never grow up.

"And inside was all Beauty and Blessedness, and Himself and I sat by Our Own Fireside and Broke Bread together before going up Our Very Own Stairs (another old custom, Journal) ——"

She pulled a piece of paper toward her, and wrote, while she thought of it, "Tell Mrs. What's-her-name must get some other kind of tea," and then went on in the Journal.

"And now it is going, this Bright and Blessed Day—how can I bear to let it go? God Bless the Days to Come, and Our Home, and Us, and our Living and our Loving, our Work and our Play, and let Peace and Happiness dwell in this House Forever!"

She had happiness at first. She loved each morning, her room fresh from just-closed windows, warm from the just-lit fire, her soft bed, her breakfast tray with thin porcelain, hot coffee, mail full of invitations. She loved putting on her new clothes and going out in her bottle-green town car to buy something for the house—a Coromandel screen, a rose-quartz Kwan-Yin, Goddess of Mercy. It made her happy to feel that through her Curtis's money, that might have been just so many sordid dollars, was being transmuted into beauty, into food for the spirit. And her new preoccupations did not make her thoughtless of others. She bought souvenirs for all the people she had not had time to remember when she was abroad —bags and scarfs for the aunts, an English pipe for Uncle Johnnie, a collar that probably really had come from Paris, for Katie Sullivan. They would never know the difference.

The dinners given in her honor by the Careys' friends were pleasant, but most of the luncheons bored her. Self-centered women, full of their own affairs. And what affairs! What shallow, surface lives they seemed to lead! It wasn't that she minded that they only thought of her as Mrs. Curtis Carey, that most of them didn't know she was Christabel Caine,

157

and, if they had known, wouldn't have cared. It was just that it made her sad for them to feel how empty their lives were of beauty, poetry, the things of the spirit. "And they exhaust me," she explained to Curtis when he tried to convince her that they were all "nice girls." "They make me long to be either alone or *real*ly with some one—the way I am really with you, darling."

But sometimes she wondered, were she and Curtis really together? He adored her, yes, but did he understand her? Or was she doomed to loneliness forever? "Tragedy, real tragedy, comes to the rare soul capable of it," she wrote in her Journal, thinking of past days when she had been really with Boyd, Gobby—Elliott. And on another day she wrote:

"To suffer! Not to dodge! To go through all pain, all sorrow! The Blessèd Angela of Foligno ——"

Was it the Blessèd Angela? She couldn't quite remember, but never mind, no one would be apt to know the difference. "The Blessèd

158

Angela of Foligno said that if pain were for sale in the market place she would run to buy it. Saint Catherine of Siena said, 'I have chosen suffering for my consolation.' 'Suffering is the ancient law of love,' said the Eternal Wisdom to Suso. 'There is no quest without pain, there is no lover who is not also a martyr.' "

With the sense of loneliness came a longing to see Elliott again, and for a time she let her imagination play with the idea. Perhaps at the theater she would glance up from her program and find him in the seat beside her, and they would look at each other with a long tranced look. Or she would step from her motor, almost in his arms. "Christabel!" And he would stand gazing at her, oblivious of passersby, until, in spite of the pain in her heart, she would have to laugh, to put her hand through his arm in the old way. Or, walking in the Park in the first snow—they had loved the first snow; they had always called it theirs—she would meet him, alone with his memories, as she was alone with hers.

But none of these dreams came true, so on a day when she had nothing that she wanted to do, and was so lonely that tears kept stinging into her eyes, she wrote asking him to tea.

As she dressed for him she paused to look deeply into the mirror, to see herself as he would see her. Head up, with gallant courage—a brave little smile. How should she greet him? What should her first words be? Perhaps a wordless welcome would be best. She went toward the mirror, both hands out. Her chiffon sleeves floated back, then fluttered down, folding wings. Gray bird, wounded bird, home in your nest again.

Her hands trembled, touching powder box and lipstick, as she remembered, shaken and glowing, that he had tried to kill himself for her. She drew a deep sobbing breath, a white hand went to her throat. Had she the courage to see him, after all? And, leaving herself out of it, was it going to be too hard for him?

But he hadn't any telephone and it was nearly tea time. And, anyway, one must not dodge life.

Oh, my dear, don't look so! Forgive you? Oh, Elliott, what is there to forgive? You have given me the greatest bliss that has entered my life, and the greatest pain, which is the same thing—how could I feel anything but love and gratitude toward you?

She opened the safe set into her blue wall, near the *prie-dieu* under an ivory Christ on an ebony cross, took out her diamond and sapphire bracelets, tried them on, then put them back again. No jewels this afternoon, except, perhaps, the triple string of pearls. Pearls are for tears.

She can't throw me over and then think all she has to do is to whistle and I'll come running, Elliott told himself, putting Christabel's note into its envelope and going back to his painting. "Oh, shut up, damn you!" he shouted at his model, a sulphur-crested cocka-

too he had borrowed from Mrs. O'Reilly on the
ground floor, that was screeching hoarsely.
I'm not going to be one of her tame young men.
He painted fiercely, biting his lower lip to keep
it from twitching. But he hardly saw what
he was painting, and the cuckatoo, still screeching, had begun to dance from one claw to the
other, to lift a yellow crest and spread a yellow-
lined wing, the quills separated, to bite with a
black beak into yellow down. It made Elliott
nervous when it behaved that way, and Christabel's note had upset him, too. The day was
ruined as far as painting went.

If he didn't go she'd think he didn't dare,
or that she had broken his heart, or something,
he told himself, pulling on a pair of thick
gloves before he offered the cockatoo a piece
of banana. "Here, pretty Cocky! *Hey!* You
will, will you, you devil? Nice birdie, have a
banana, and then we'll go down to Mrs.
O'Reilly."

Coming back to peace and quiet, he reread
her note. "Elliott—please come—" she had

written after her signature, and the letters looked not quite steady.

Was he or was he not a man of the world? That was the question, he decided. After all, one evolved a philosophy of life that kept one from taking oneself or anyone else too seriously. He wrote, saying that he would come, and then went out to buy a necktie.

The next afternoon he dressed with fingers that trembled, in spite of the cynical smile reflected in his mirror. Perhaps it was all for the best—one evolves a philosophy of life. He retied his tie—worse than the last time!

Pulling at it, a sudden panic seized him. He would have given anything not to go. He could telephone from the drug store—but what could he say? Suppose he just stayed here, and sent her a note tomorrow saying he had been taken ill or suddenly called out of town?

She was expecting him. He couldn't disappoint her.

Gobby had reported her as bitterly unhappy in Paris. Suppose seeing him was too much for her? Had he any right to expose her to such an emotional strain?

And yet, if he could comfort her ——

What, crying? Silly little Christabel!

Damn! A hole in his heel. Maybe it wouldn't show over the top of his shoe.

He began to feel forgiving, protective. Christabel, dearest girl, what is there to forgive?

Some one had told him about a man who had killed himself for Christabel, taking poison on the day of her wedding. There were not many girls for whom men would kill themselves. And this girl, who, in the world's eyes, had everything, needed him—had sent for him.

He wondered who the poor fellow had been.

Her house, washed pink, with twisted columns, and a noseless saint in a niche above the door, was so Venetian that a gondola should have been before it instead of the delivery motor of The Superior Market, Third Avenue. He gave his name scornfully, with drooping mouth and eyelids, throwing away his hat and

164

stick. The butler caught them, and led him through thick fog to the drawing room, leaving him there to wait for Christabel.

He waited.

The fog began to lift. He looked about him. Things, material possessions! Only a bird in a gilded cage, he sang in his mind with bitter mirth, for he and Donatia and Boyd and Gobby were finding old songs rather amusing that autumn. A butler, tapestries, silver and lace on the table before the fire—what an absurd scale of values they implied. And yet there were people who were impressed by such things.

Poor Christabel. So she has come to this, he thought, contrasting the huge sheaves of chrysanthemums like helpings of crab salad, the Madonna drenched in brown gravy, with that other firelit room of hers, exquisite and simple —one perfect rose, his portrait of her alone on the wall.

Was she coming? No, not yet. But his heart began to thud. What should his first words be? He adjusted his tie in the glass over the dark Madonna.

Footsteps outside the door. Heavens! He hoped he wasn't going to be sick!

She came toward him with both hands out. Her chiffon sleeves floated behind her. How lovely she was! They looked at each other deeply, until they were interrupted by the footman bringing in tea.

"So good of you to suggest my coming."

"So good of you to *come*. Cigarette?" And, as the footman left the room, "Now tell me— everything."

"What is there to tell that you don't already know?"

"Sometimes I feel as if I didn't know anything, Elliott—or at least that I hadn't known anything until it was too late to be of any use. Do you ever feel that way?"

"All I've learned is that nothing's worth being unhappy about," said Elliott, with a laugh so scornful and explosive that it startled himself.

166

"Oh, my dear, not that, not that! Don't let it make you bitter!"

The footman brought in crumpets, and Christabel began to pour Elliott's tea. He watched her put in lemon, and said nothing, though he always took cream. Their hands shook so as she gave him the cup that tea splashed out and scalded him. How sad her face was! He asked, for the footman's ears:

"Did you have a wonderful trip?"

"Did I? Why, yes—yes, of course we did."

"Where did you go?"

"Oh, the usual places. London and Paris and motoring through the château country."

The footman went out.

"Christabel, are you happy? Forgive me, I have to know!"

"Is *any*one happy, Elliott? Well, I suppose a good many are, really—at least, they aren't sensitive enough for anything but cowlike content—but that isn't what you and I mean by happiness, is it?"

"Oh, Christabel, why ——?"

The footman brought in cakes.

"Are you writing anything now?"

"I'm just getting back to it. There have been so many interruptions. Are you painting?"

The footman put another log on the fire.

"That will do, Alfred, thank you. And I'm not at home to anyone."

Now that the man was gone, Elliott wasn't sure what to say. Everything he could think of seemed too much or too little. They drank their tea in silence, gazing into the fire. And he was horrified to realize that he had absent-mindedly eaten all his crumpet. He hoped Christabel wouldn't notice or would think he hadn't taken one. It looked so unfeeling. And yet, after all, why should he worry about seeming unfeeling to her, who had been so unfeeling herself? He took another crumpet defiantly.

"Elliott—I must say something to you— quickly, now, while I have the courage. I must tell you that I think I must have been mad when I did what I did. I don't understand why I did it—it wasn't love, unless compassion is love, and pity—he seemed to *need* me so! And you only seemed to need your work —— No, no, don't speak. Let me finish before my courage fails me! A woman wants so terribly to be *need*ed, Elliott."

Her hand lay white on the dark velvet between them. He lifted it to his lips. How good it smelled!

"You asked me if I were happy, but I don't believe you, being you, need to have me tell you. But what does that matter? One learns how unimportant one's own happiness is."

"Yes, the important thing is accepting life."

"*Isn't* it? Oh, how true that is! If only we didn't have to suffer so to learn it!"

She pressed a lace-bordered cobweb to her eyes, and then smiled at him.

"More tea? I'm not a very good hostess, am I? A little pink cake, specialty of the house? Oh, Elliott, do you remember going to the *pâtisserie* to get cakes for tea?"

"Do I! And our discussions in front of the

169

fire? You and I settling life and death, while Gobby finished up the pastry?"

"Oh, Elliott, teach me to be brave like you! Because I do know how brave you are—I don't mean just in being able to laugh, dear, I mean —I—I just want you to know—I know!"

Know what? he wondered, holding her hands in his, while he wondered, too, what time Mr. Carey got home. It would be just as well to be gone by then.

"And I do realize the courage it takes—just to live. I do understand, because on the ship —I wouldn't tell this to anyone else in the world, but I owe it to you—the water seemed to call me. I was so tired, it would have been so easy! But I *had* to tell you, so that you would know I understand, and know how I thank you and how proud I am of you, and how grateful I am that what happened happened!"

She's overwrought, he thought. Seeing me has been too much for her. "I'd better go," he said, struggling up from the soft low sofa.

"Yes, perhaps it would be better."

"Good-by."

"Good-by, my dear."

Her hand fluttered to her throat, her fingers twisted nervously through strands of pearls.

"Elliott—I must say one thing more to you before you go. Never blame yourself for anything that has happened. You have given me the greatest bliss that I have ever known, and the greatest pain, which is the same thing— how can I ever feel anything but love and gratitude toward you?"

"Oh, Christabel ——

"You must go now, Elliott."

He was thrilled, his whole body tingled as he lifted a floating sleeve to his lips. Courage and love and sorrow. Elliott and Christabel.

"And do one thing for me, my dear. Forget what I have told you, and when you think of me—*if* you think of me—think that I am happy ——"

Chapter Thirteen

In Christabel's old room Mrs. Caine was painting tea trays with baskets of flowers for the Hospital Fair. The forget-me-nots were the most fun to do, dot, dot, dot, dot with the pale blue paint, then one dot of yellow in the center. As she painted she wrote a letter in her head. Darling Christabel—Guess what I have been doing all afternoon? Painting! You didn't know I was an artist, did you? I have been painting trays for the Fair, and really if I do say it they are just as pretty as can be. I am doing them with little baskets of flowers——

Dot, dot, dot, dot. Thursday. Katie's day out, but it was never any trouble to get supper for Fred. She was just going to have deviled crabs; they were all ready to pop into the oven. There was a Mary Pickford picture to go to later. Life is full of nice things, she thought, glowing. Deviled crabs, movies, Fred, my painting ——

She finished a tray, and had a good look at it, pleased and surprised that she had done anything so charming. A vague plan of painting all the bedroom furniture with bunches of old-fashioned flowers drifted through her mind. She began another tray, humming a song.

> "*And* for mm-hmm *dum*-dee *Lau*rie,
> I'd lay-*hee* hmm-*hmm* dum-dee hmm!"

Through the open window came the sound of Jake's lawn-mower, the scent of freshly cut grass. Another scent, that always brought memories of a child's summer by the sea, the scent of privet flowers hot in the sun. She entered the tiny shop—boxes of glass beads, blue, green, gold, and coral-color—peppermint hearts with "Ever Thine" and "Kiss And Make Up" on them in bright pink—dolls with shiny black china hair and tiny feet in high black china boots. She was on the beach where shells holding a little sand and water lay half buried

173

in wet sand. She popped blisters in brown sea-weed between thumb and finger; she felt sand between her toes again.

Was that an automobile stopping? The maple tree had grown against the window, so she could no longer see the gate. Yes, the door bell—bother! I'll just let it ring, she said, but she knew she would answer it.

"Mother!"

"*Christ*abel! *Da*rling! Where on earth did you come from? Jake! Oh, Jake! Carry Miss Christabel's bag upstairs, please. Darling, why didn't you let us know you were coming? Katie's out, and everything. Never mind, it's lovely to see you. Everything's all right, isn't it?"

"Everything's all wrong; that's why I came."

"But——?"

"No, I don't mean that. Of course everything's all right."

"But what——?"

"Please, mother darling! I don't want to

174

talk about it, if you don't mind. How are you?"

"I'm fine."

"*Are* you?"

"Don't I look it?"

"You look sweet. But I'm very much afraid you're naughty, now that I'm not here to look after you. Haven't you been overdoing? You look tired to me, dear. You *must* remember that you can't do all the things you used to do."

"Oh, I'm all right." But for the first time she noticed that her back was aching—well, not exactly aching, but she could feel it. That was because she had been transplanting seedlings all morning. She wouldn't mention that, for Christabel had never understood how anyone could really enjoy working in a garden.

She did feel tired, now that she stopped to think about it. But, thank goodness, the guest room was ready. All she had to do was get out the sandal-wood soap, from Christmas, the best bureau cover, and embroidered towels.

"Oh, mother! You're not going to make

company of me and put me in the guest room?
Oh no! Just put me in my own old room.
I've come home to be your little girl again, and
try to forget things."

"Well, but it's in an awful mess. I've been
painting tea trays. See!" She held up the best
one proudly.

"Mother! Aren't you cunning? They're
*love*ly tea trays, simply *love*ly!"

Feeling like a foolish child, Mrs. Caine
carried out the trays, while Christabel shed her
clothes.

"Mercy, it's hot! Don't bother about fixing
things up, mother dear. Oh, mother, I want
to pretend I'm just the way I used to be, that
I've never been away—I want to forget everything——"

"Christabel dearest, I'm so worried about
you. Couldn't you tell me what's the matter?
Perhaps I could help."

"No, darling, I'm not going to have you
bothered, too."

"It isn't—you haven't—Curtis——?"

176

"Curtis is happy and well, and it isn't, and I haven't. Now we'll just forget about it."

"But ——"

"Now sit right down here. Mother, how long since you've seen a doctor?"

"Goodness! I can't remember! Ages."

"I want you to promise me to go and see Dr. Henderson. No, I know, there isn't anything the matter with you, and you're strong as a prize-fighter, *but*, all the same, I want you to promise to see Dr. Henderson. It's just common sense to have a good overhauling now and then, as one gets older. I can't have anything happening to my little mother!"

She kissed her tenderly.

"I have a little present for you."

Mrs. Caine, who had begun to droop, revived, and thought hopefully of chocolates. Christabel shook out an orchid-satin bed-jacket edged with uncurled ostrich in long waving fronds.

"There! It's to tempt you to have your breakfasts in bed and save yourself a little."

"It's lovely! And, oh, dear, I'm afraid it must have been terribly expensive!"

"It wasn't cheap," Christabel admitted, smiling, and then suddenly cried:

"Oh, mother, if I only had a child! You don't know, you can't even imagine, the sorrow of childlessness! Oh, if I only had a little daughter to comfort me!"

But she got hold of herself again in a minute, after she had clung half weeping to her mother, and went to take a bath.

Oh, dear! What *is* the matter? thought Mrs. Caine, squatting slowly to pick up lace and ribbons, putting her hand to her back as she rose. Just like old times to be picking up after Christabel. It's a lucky thing for her she has a maid.

How hot it was getting! Breathless! And it had been so lovely.

That bed-jacket was beautiful, and it was darling of Christabel to have brought it to her, but she never had her breakfasts in bed; she couldn't, with one girl, and Fred would think

178

she was ill. Perhaps she could wear it down-stairs to breakfast sometimes—but it would make her feel shy and silly, and she could see the ostrich fronds getting into coffee and but-ter.

If only Christabel had telegraphed ahead! Then her room would have been all ready, and Katie could have gone out on Wednesday ——

Goodness! Not a thing in the house for dessert! She went to the telephone and called her husband.

"Fred! Christabel's here. . . . No, I didn't know. . . . No—no, I don't know for how long. I'm very much worried. . . . I said I was worried. . . . I can't tell you now. . . . I said never mind now—but, Fred, listen, I haven't anything for dessert. Would you just stop at Bent's and bring home a quart and a pint of strawberry ice-cream? . . . No, they won't deliver this late—they'll put it in a nice container—a quart and a pint of strawberry. . . . I don't think so at all. Why on earth *should* she let us know?   If our own child can't come home any time she wants to ——!"

Relieved by Fred's saying he thought Christabel might have telegraphed ahead, she left the telephone to answer Christabel, calling from upstairs.

"Mother!   If you *are* coming upstairs any time—don't make a special trip, but just *when* you do—*would* you bring me a bowl of ice?"

It really is getting hotter and hotter, Mrs. Caine thought, running out to the garden to cut roses for the table, pausing to wipe her forehead with the back of her wrist, opening the emergency bottle of olives because Christabel was used to grandeur now, shutting the refrigerator lid on her finger.   Only the thought of the ice-cream Fred had brought sustained her.   But when it appeared, Christabel said she was dieting, and might she have just a little fruit?

Mrs. Caine agitatedly poked into the refrigerator.   One banana, but Christabel didn't like bananas much, and, besides, this really was too black for anything.   A cantaloupe. . She

180

could have half of that for tonight, and half for breakfast. Mrs. Caine would make her stay in bed, so she shouldn't see that they weren't having cantaloupe, too. Fred didn't like bananas, either. Well, she would eat that, and he would just have to do with the saucer of stewed rhubarb she saw lurking behind the box of eggs and the left-over custard. And all the time, as she hurried to get the cantaloupe ready, she got hotter and hotter, and she could feel the ice-cream melting away, exactly as if she were it, going all shapeless and soft.

After supper she rather timidly suggested the movies.

"Of course, dear, if you want to."

"But would *you* like to? It's Mary Pickford!"

"*Is* it? Mother, you are too darling!"

"I just thought you might enjoy it——"

But, although Christabel was sweet about it, they didn't go. They sat on the porch, looking at fireflies, and asking Christabel respectful questions about the book she was at work on.

It was the story of an exquisite girl, married to one man, loved by another. Her husband didn't even try to understand her, and she loved the other man, but he was the one she was going to send away. Mrs. Caine approved of that, though she was disappointed to hear that the book was to end unhappily. She thought Christabel might have let the husband die. How interesting to hear about her books even before they're written, Mrs. Caine thought, giving way to a wide yawn in the dark, and then suddenly cried:

"*Christ*abel! Coffee! I forgot! We've sort of gotten out of the way of having it, since you left. Father thought it kept him awake, and it seemed silly to have it just for me. But I'll make some right away."

"*Don't* bother about coffee, mother."

"But you always have it at your house."

"That doesn't mean I have to have it here."

But she went in and made it.

After she had taken the cups back to the kitchen, and had a secret, guilty peep at the

182

evening paper there, she slipped up to turn down Christabel's bed and put out her fragrant cobweb nightgown. What beautiful things her child owned! Tortoise shell, crystal stoppered with gold, the little heaps of flexible diamond and sapphire bracelets she had pulled off because they made her wrist hot, and that made Mrs. Caine feel watching eyes in every shadow in the room.

From the porch she could hear Fred. "What does Curtis think——?" And Christabel's answering murmur. Her dear little girl. It was lovely to have her home. But what was troubling her? Every time the telephone rang —and it had rung several times this evening— she had jumped, her hand had flown to her heart. I wish she'd tell me. But she doesn't want to worry me—she's very thoughtful.

She could smell honeysuckle. It made her feel sad. Long, long ago; long, long ago. You smell honeysuckle by night, and privet by day when the sun is on it.

What had she been thinking of just as

Christabel came? Something that had made her feel so happy—it was just on the tip of her mind——

No, she couldn't remember.

Pausing by the bureau to turn out the light, she looked into the mirror. She did look tired. Tired and old.

Christabel went to bed early. It was relaxing to put on her old wrapper, still in the closet, plaster on cold cream, and read *The Ladies' Home Journal.* "How wonderfully she comes home!" she could hear people saying. "Just like a little girl again—completely unspoiled." I'm glad I've kept my love for simple things, she thought, lighting another cigarette.

Home was rather pleasant, after all, with its shabby chintz and shabby old books, and garden roses whose edges had been nibbled by insects. Dinner starting right in without any soup, and the tablecloth just a tablecloth, not a bishop's brocaded robe or a lace altar cloth. She was glad she had been thoughtful enough

184

to come without letting them know ahead—it had saved them all bother of preparation. She knew her mother! She would have hurried around getting flowers and making chocolate cake, and there would have been chicken for dinner because of company. For that matter, she would be surprised if there weren't chicken and chocolate cake tomorrow. She would remember never to let them know. Happy surprises were so good for people.

Poor darling little mother! If only she didn't *need* me so!

Life was a heavy load. She had tried to run away from her own trouble, but here it was, sighing in the leaves outside her window, filling the familiar room, rolling her from side to side in her bed, as waves roll a pebble.

She tried to remember her letter. Elliott dear, my heart is breaking with what I have to write to you. Why must we always give each other the terrible gift of pain? How can I say what I must say to you? Then what? She couldn't remember exactly, but she had written that they had better stop seeing each other.

Dear Elliott, she would always love him, of course. Shutting her eyes, she could make herself see, with almost no effort at all, small bright pictures of herself and him—at least, she usually could, but tonight the porter on the train from New York melted into Curtis practicing an approach shot on her hearth-rug while he told her to have a good time; Curtis melted into the sweet peas on her dressing-table. She must be more exhausted than she had realized. She yawned until there was a roaring in her ears.

But the situation had become strained. Elliott was demanding too much, expecting to come to tea all the time, and turning sulky if anyone else was there. All winter, all spring, their tragedy had flooded her life with melancholy interest; she had thrilled to his adoration. Somehow all her circle had gotten to know about it, except, of course, Curtis, if he counted as one of her circle. They had made her feel glamorous with love and sorrow. It has been a beautiful winter, for all its pain, she thought. But now she felt that he and she must part, for his own sake, and she had written him so. She had told him not to come again. What if it does bring me loneliness, utter loneliness? she thought, crushing out her cigarette and turning off the light. No one shall know. I have no right to make others unhappy just because my own heart is aching. She saw herself a gallant lady, smiling, smiling —— She really did see herself, in a green velvet riding-habit, the skirt lifted by a delicate gauntleted hand, a plumed hat shading the lovely tragic eyes, the smiling mouth, like a lady in an old painting. The Gallant Lady.

Three days ago she had written him, telling him there was no possible answer. And then she had waited for his answer until today, when, in a panic of nervousness, she had run away home. With his tendency to suicide, suppose it had been too much for him. Every time the telephone rang she had nearly died. Oh,

I'm so tired, so tired, she thought. I don't want to see him, or hear from him—I don't want to think about him ——

With a sudden feeling of suction in her chest, she thought, suppose he does kill himself this time, and suppose my letters are found. Suppose they get into the papers, for Curtis to read. What had she written? *What* had she written? Dozens of notes ——

Oh, Curtis, she thought, it's you I love, my dear. So strong, so safe. It's to you I give all my loyalty.

If I'm ever such a fool as to get into a mess like this again ——!

Try to relax. Think of something pleasant. Gerald Smith. She had seen him in the train coming out to Germantown, and had promised to lunch with him in Philadelphia tomorrow. She tingled, remembering the way he had looked at her.

Darling mother and father! She must come home oftener. And yet that meant loneliness for her own dear Curtis.

188

Those touching little trays—her breakfast on a tray—she supposed she would have to have it, it would make mother so happy. My dear, I only want you to be happy, truly, truly, it doesn't matter about me. No, she mustn't let herself think about Elliott.

A sighing in the leaves deepened to a delicate patter, the sleepy sound of rain flowed through the darkness. What is he thinking now, lying awake? The grass and wildflowers will root in this aching heart, this tired brain—remember that, use it sometime. The grass will break my heart and pierce my side—Jake cutting grass—father and mother must have the privet hedge cut; it looks awful, all overgrown, nobody lets privet bloom—Gerald—tomorrow—mother's chocolate cake—Gerald, dear, please, you mustn't say things like that —Gerald——

Chapter Fourteen

CHRISTABEL was discontented and restless in the months that followed her dismissal of Elliott. Not because she missed him. It was a relief to have him out of her life, for he had begun to be unmanageable. She wanted to be adored. She wanted to prove almost too much for men, to make them love her passionately and almost uncontrollably, in spite of all her efforts to save them. To feel that they were always just about to burst, but never quite bursting, that she was to them not only a woman, but a high star. She basked in an atmosphere of reverent passion as sweet and warm as the atmosphere of her firelit flower-filled rooms, and the fires of love were as well controlled as the fires in her fireplaces, that Alfred kept supplied with logs, and screened when sparks began to fly.

Most of her adorers were willing coöperators. They were dramatic young men, who could throw themselves into their parts so fully that they themselves believed in their firmly closed lips, their dilated nostrils. She and the young man of the moment spoke to each other fragmentarily, their words, she thought, like sunbright leaves floating lightly on deep waters. The Tuesday young man who had done his drawing room in solferino velvet, with beadwork bell-pulls, and wreaths under glass of straw-colored ferns and dark blackberries made from hair; the Friday young man who had designed the curious costumes for the Monday young man's play in which a murderer fell in love with a wax saint. There were mild thrills sometimes as hand touched hand when cups were refilled. But when the soft collars and pastel-tinted neckties were gone, they left no troubled wake, nothing more upset than the crushed silk cushions, the two half-empty teacups, the pile of cigarette stubs, that showed some one else had been understanding Christabel.

But Elliott had shown signs of forgetting to

be reverent to an exhausting degree, and was only kept in order by the more exhausting means of being led to talk exclusively about himself and his painting. When she said those things that demanded wordless answers, restraint shown by clenched hand or bitten lip, he was increasingly apt to answer literally. She was glad, for both their sakes, that she had been strong enough to decide they should not see each other again. That was not why she was so depressed. She did not know the cause, she could not find a cure.

She was bored with theaters, bored with dinners; she wept when Curtis suggested Florida. In her mother-in-law's box at the opera, lent them week after week, drifting her feather fan through air vibrating with plump Mimi's last farewells, kilted Edgardo's laments, or the love-making of Pinkerton and Cho-Cho-San, she was so bored she could have screamed. Amusements can't help me, she thought. People can't help me. Yet somewhere there must be

192

a still peace where I can be lost, and find myself again.

She thought of God. She would become one with God.

She had always suspected herself of the mystical temperament. Now she took up contemplation, gazing at an apple until she became one with it, the apple blossom within it that had changed to a star, the seeds, little brown monks in their cells, the dark roots, the branches melting into light, the cycle of the seasons. If I can see this clearly, I can see God, she told herself. One of her best-known poems sprang from that apple she took from the silver fruit dish, wedding gift of Mr. and Mrs. Talbot Emery Towne.

She found she could practice contemplation on anything, a walnut that became a fairy shallop with a wrinkled passenger, a sweet pea, mauve wings netted in green tendrils, rimmed with celestial glory. Even hard things —alley cats, telegraph poles. She was delighted to find that she could see the light of heaven pulsing through them all.

Meditation, too. That was harder, because her thoughts became a swarm of bees when she tried to empty her mind, to hold to the central silence. "Take your seat within the heart of the thousand-petaled lotus," she read in an Eastern book brought her by Gobby, who was charmed by her new ideas, and all for companionably contemplating and meditating with her. And though she wished the words hadn't reminded her of an invitation to mount a sight-seeing bus, she found them helpful. She could see the thousand up-curling petals; from the tip of each she could see pure light pouring toward the core of incredible brightness that was herself, sitting cross-legged in the golden heart. Being still, listening for the inner voice, she would think, Who of the rest of the people I know is doing anything like this?

God helped her to write *Fly in Amber* that winter. Each night she placed the next few pages of her novel in His hands. She had never written so easily.

The nights were best of all. Lying in her soft bed under linen and lace and silk, she gave herself up to the life of the spirit. Only to lose myself utterly, utterly, she thought, floating light and warm in the darkness. Only to rid myself of self, to be utterly Thine. Oh, Perfect Love, fill me and flood me! I am a shell that holds the sound of the sea, I am a raindrop that holds the sky and the stars. Come to me, Lover and Beloved. She would lie still, trembling, half-fainting. Sometimes, if she could keep still long enough, light spattered, scarlet or white, on the blackness of closed lids, and in a panic she would jerk herself back to consciousness, her heart pounding. Gobby agreed with her that she had been in great and glorious danger. He had not progressed beyond swimming yellow polka dots, and then he was always distracted by something —a taxi, a blanket tickling him.

In her Secret Journal she described her new absorption.

"To be rid of Self—to cast my Self into the white-hot flame of Thy Love, and be consumed."

And again:

"Oh, happy-torment that Thou givest me! Oh, tide of Love and Blessing and Brightness that Thou pourest into me, and through poor little me into the World! And yet I won't say, poor little me, but Blessed Me, because Thou hast deigned to make me part of Thee, to choose me for Thy Beloved——"

These entries seemed rather daring when she read them over, remembering the religion of Dr. Marsh and the congregation in Germantown. Kid gloves, oak pews, green and purple shepherds in memorial windows, hymn 505, the Glory of God bounded by late breakfast with pancakes, by mid-day dinner with roast beef. She could not imagine Dr. Marsh with his glittering cuffs and broad As, or Mrs. Marsh with her feather boa and her pince-nez, shuddering with ecstasy beneath the Divine caresses, or approving of the shudders of any of their flock. But beside the books on mysticism her words were mild. Other people, if they were writing the truth, had been through even more intense experiences than she, and were outspoken in their descriptions. Determinedly she resumed her seat in the heart of the thousand-petaled lotus.

Sometimes her nights of ecstasy left her half-sick and dizzy in the morning. Even when she found it more and more necessary to pump up her interest in the life of the spirit, the sickness and dizziness remained. Her restlessness returned, she repeated to herself again and again what she had said to her mother—if I only had a child!

On her bedside table, with *The Imitation of Christ* and *The Little Flowers of Saint Francis* (she must remember to cut the pages! Often after she had gone to bed she would have picked it up, except for that) she placed a baby's dimpled hand in alabaster, and some-

197

times when she looked at it tears rose to her eyes, surprising her a little, touching her deeply. Children playing in the Park caused her to weep, and she wrote in her Journal:

"When I walk, my Little Dream Boy runs by my side ——"

Some of her most poignant poems were written that winter, on the sorrow of childlessness.

She got into such a low state of mind that Curtis finally persuaded her to see Dr. Deacon.

After the doctor left she lay thinking of what he had told her. In her windows pots of hyacinths with close-packed buds split the pale spring sunshine. It was the first day of April.

April Fool's Day. Her eyes fell on the baby's alabaster hand by her bed, and she gave it a slight push and turned her head away.

Lying there in her white-lace nightgown, under blue coverlet with silver stars, she felt herself floating, a cloud in the sky, a disembodied spirit. She crossed her hands, arching the delicate wrists, and closed her eyes, and she could see herself lying there as if she stood

198

by her own bed. She could see tall white candles with golden flames, a pall of white narcissus, golden-hearted. A voice said, "So young, in all the promise of her genius!" Another voice answered, "Her poor little mother-less baby ——" A tear oozed from her closed lids—another ——

But Curtis, on his knees by her bed, was adoring and delighted. His family and her family petted and praised her. She had never been given so many presents. A new car, strands of pearls for her wrists, the enormous emerald held in a circle of frost that she had fallen in love with at Cartier's and that Curtis had said he couldn't afford.

Her mother wrote:

"Uncle Johnnie complains that he can't take a step in any of the aunts' houses without getting a loop of pink wool around his ankle, they are all so busy knitting socks and sacques for the darling baby."

The two families worshiped her, solicitous, until they made her feel like a young Madonna rising starry with hope and fear from the dark kneeling circle.

"After all, what career is as great as motherhood?" she asked Boyd Benjamin, who had dropped in for a whisky and soda and to deplore this handicap to Christabel's career.

"I knew it! I knew when you married uptown and got prosperous that you'd go Victorian, too."

"Victoria didn't invent having babies."

"Specious," said Boyd, screwing a cigarette into a foot-long holder.

"To give life isn't a little thing, Boyd; it's a very beautiful and wonderful privilege," Christabel said, gently, and she thought, Frustration! That's what it is. Frustration and subconscious jealousy. Poor old Boyd! Then, as Boyd continued to scowl and puff, regardless of Christabel's hand waving away the smoke or pressing a handkerchief to her nose, she added:

"Boyd darling, *would* you mind not smoking? I *hate* to stop you, but one gets silly when one's not very strong——"

Poor Boyd! she's getting—well, the only word is coarse—she thought, letting the smoke curl lazily from her nostrils, resting after Boyd had gone. But it's hard on people whose lack of appeal keeps them outside the stream of life. Poor old Boyd, worrying about careers, as if painting eggplants, or even writing poems, mattered at all compared with being what was really the heart of the world, a mother.

She could not help realizing that the Secret Journal touched heights during those months that it had never touched before, could not help believing that when it was published—if it was published—years and years away—those letters in it to her unborn child would comfort and inspire other women, would speak softly as opening petals and clearly as trumpets. Not to mention the poems that made up "First Born"——"Out of the whirlwind I gathered the small white Flower," "Mystery, small as a seed and more great than the Sun," and the rest.

In November her twins were born, strong and beautiful.

She named them Michael and Marigold, expecting opposition, but the names charmed everyone. Uncle Johnnie was reported as pretending to think they were called Patrick and Petunia, but nothing was sacred to Uncle Johnnie.

Toward the end of her convalescence she granted an audience to Gobby. Coming noiselessly to the door of her sitting room, she found him with his back to her, bending, scooping up something—what on earth was he doing? Then she realized he was practicing kissing a hand of air, and, tactfully withdrawing, made a more audible entrance, and received on her own hand the result of his practice.

"Christabel, I didn't think you could be more beautiful, but you are. I'm not being personal!"

"Dear Gobby! It's wonderful to see you again."

"That Madonna-blue chiffon! And the way

202

the light falls behind your head actually makes a sort of halo."

She smiled on her worshiper, letting her hand rest lightly on his arm.

"You mustn't spoil me!"

"No one could do that!"

"What is this intriguing parcel?"

"Some Balkan toys for the babies."

"Gobby, how divine! Oh! This shell-pink pig is my favorite, *so* corpulent! So exactly like you! To find such entrancing things, I mean. And *oh*, this gnome in the pine-cone hat! How the *Wunderkinder* will adore them, after a while! Oh, Gobby, how I do long to have you see my two absurd kitten-eyed angels! But Miss Hess hardly lets *me* look at them. A strawberry tart? I had Mrs. Britton make them especially for you."

"Christabel, I do think having a cook you call Mrs. is just the height of style! I really am touched. I believe you remember my weakness for strawberry tarts from the Gay Street days! That reminds me, I didn't tell you about Elliott and Donatia, did I?"

"What about Elliott and Donatia?"

"Well, I think it really is going to happen this time—I think they really are going to get married. They're together the whole time. Of course it's almost happened so many times, but this time does seem different."

"Does he seem happy?"

"He certainly does! I think it would be fine, don't you?"

"I want Elliott to be happy almost more than I want anything in the world, Gobby. *I* can't see happiness for him with Donatia, but perhaps you're right. I hope so, with all my heart."

After he went she lay thinking of what he had told her. Elliott and Donatia. Elliott and Do*natia!* Really!

I didn't think you could be more beautiful, but you are. Gobby's voice sounded through her thoughts. She did feel slender and beautiful again. Getting up, she clasped her hands

204

behind her head, then ran them down her sides. Beautiful, a mirror repeated.

Deceived by her courage, the specialists, Dr. Train and Dr. Von Boden, with Dr. Deacon a weak echo, had told Curtis she had had an unusually easy time. She would never trust any of them again. She had come through the Valley of the Shadow of Death. She ought to know. It was she who had had the twins. But now her body was humming with life, she wanted to live again with all her being.

She gazed at her reflection. I didn't think you could be more beautiful, but you are. I've been to a dark place and a far place—unimaginable awfulness—Elliott and Donatia— shadows in blue chiffon—I've come back wiser. I didn't think you could be more beautiful ——

Going to her desk, she took a sheet of her special paper, with *Christabel* in her handwriting flung in a silver spray across a corner, and wrote:

ELLIOTT DEAR:

I've been to a dark place and a far place since we last saw each other. And now that it's over—the unimaginable awfulness—I would not for anything give it up, for I've come back stronger and wiser. I've come back knowing that loving-kindness from friend to friend is the only thing that really matters, I've come back longing—longing—to see the few I really care for.

Will you come and see me?

CHRISTABEL.

Chapter Fifteen

T HE United States entered the World War with Christabel's complete approval. Yet her patriotism did not make her narrow-minded. She was able to assure Elliott, a pacifist, that she understood why he refused to stand up in theaters when the "Star-spangled Banner" was played. "I do, I do understand so completely how much more courage it takes than it would to fight, how much easier it would be to join in the war hysteria, and I honor you for it," she told him, at the same time that she told him she couldn't go to the theater with him that evening.

Friends who were in New York were being kind to her in the evenings, trying to keep her from being lonely, for Curtis, beautiful in uniform, had left for a South Carolina camp.

"The poetry was lovely," he wrote Christabel. "And I am certainly looking forward to reading the book on Spiritual Values just

as soon as I get time." And a page later,
"Could you send me some detective books, as
I have quite a lot of time on my hands?"

Gobby was a sergeant, somewhere in France.
"The poetry was wonderful," he wrote Christabel. "I feel from it that you must be suffering exquisitely, and my only consolation is that
it is marvelous for your art. I will write you
my reactions to the essays on Spiritual Values
just as soon as I get time to read them—they
keep us pretty busy here, as you can imagine!
Since you are so sweet as to ask if there is anything else I would like to have you send me, I
would certainly love some chocolate. You have
to be a millionaire when it comes to buying it
here ——"

Boyd Benjamin was in France, driving an
ambulance. Christabel could see her, in the
unbecoming mud and mustard of her khaki uniform, striding along with steps twice as long
as any man's, and following that vision she
could see herself, in white that turned from
silver to gold as she went down a long corridor,

in and out of sunlight falling from high windows. She saw the faces on the pillows brighten. "Sister ——" "Sister ——" Even the most terribly wounded managed to whisper it as she passed, managed a twisted answering smile to her smile that was so near tears.

But she did not go to France. "I long to go—oh, how I long to go!" she told Austin Weeks, who in happier days had done the portrait of her in a gray velvet *robe de style*, with a greyhound curled about her, that hung over Curtis's desk and who now was camouflaging battle-ships in the Brooklyn Navy Yard. "But I know the biggest sacrifice I can make for our boys is to stay here and use my own special gift, just as you are doing. Anyone can drive an ambulance, or nurse, but we who have been given gifts—oh, Austin, are we blessed or cursed?——we have no choice."

So, although she did a little work in a white uniform and veil—the costume she wore in the beautiful photographs used to advertise her book of war poems—and gave a great deal of

Curtis's money, she felt that her important work was in connection with her writing. She autographed hundreds of copies of books for bazaars; *Fly in Amber*, selling well, supported several war orphans; and she never said no to a request for a benefit reading. Two or three times a week she could be seen coming out of her Venetian house, a Venetian lady in a black tricorne, with a small black lace mask of veil shading her mysterious eyes, going to read her poems somewhere. "Perhaps they will comfort some one just a little," she said, wistfully.

"It seems to me so wrong not to try to bring as much beauty into this poor ugly world as you can, *especially* now," she said to Austin Weeks. "I feel as if, just *because* my own heart is so heavy—oh, Austin, so heavy, so heavy!—I must make an effort, now of all times, to try to look as nice as I can." And to his answer she had to reply: "Oh, Austin, you mustn't talk like that! You mustn't spoil me!"

So when she read before clubs and circles,

or sat at speakers' tables, she wore soft fur and velvet and pearls, and sometimes overheard, among the people crowding around to meet her, a whispered:

"She's like a little queen!"

And she tried to be queenly, in the highest sense—*Noblesse oblige*—to her adorers as they were introduced.

"Oh, Miss Caine! This is a *real* privilege! I don't know whether you caught my name. I'm Mrs. Merkle, Grace Gladwin Merkle, you might possibly have heard it in connection with my talks on 'The Psychology of Success.' I wanted to tell you how interested I was in *Fly in Amber*, it had a theme so like a novel I wrote several years ago—well, no, it wasn't published, but several publishers considered it ——"

"Oh, Mrs. Caine, your reading was *simply* marvelous!"

"*This* isn't Christabel Caine? But, my dear, you're only a child!"

"This is a *great* pleasure, Miss Caine! I'm

sure you must be tired of hearing how much we all enjoyed your poems! I wonder if you ever happened to meet my nephew—he's a poet, too —Edgar Temple Anderson—well, it's a little volume called *Heart's Home*, and then he won the Southwestern Poetry Society's second prize with a poem called 'Mary Magdalene on Broadway' ——"

"I just can't tell you ——"

"Your poems were delightful, Miss Caine."

"I enjoyed your reading particularly, Miss Caine, being a writer myself ——"

Poor dears, thought Christabel, hearing her voice answer their adulation graciously, gently. After all, how human to try to shine, even if it's only by reflected light. Amusing, and pitiful, and yet rather beautiful. It was like something Austin Weeks had said, that had struck her as so true, "Life is the laughter of a broken-hearted clown."

She wrote in her Secret Journal:

"No one will ever know how hard these readings are. They leave me utterly spent, and

212

wimple of white crêpe framing the lovely oval of her face, she looked like a young Mother Superior. "Precious person!" the lady next Uncle Johnnie groaned, and her companion whispered reverently, "War widow?" while other ladies whispered, "Shsh!" for Christabel had begun to read.

You win, Christabel, Uncle Johnnie thought. No matter what the circumstances, I back you to win!

"I will not speak of these things, let me keep
   Silence to cloak my wounds—the tears that I
Have shed for you, the passionate and deep
   Blue of the gentian under the sad sky ——"

Christabel was reading, and much more to the same effect—a thorough inventory, ending:

   "Of these, while still I live, I will not speak."

Quite right, too, thought Uncle Johnnie. Don't you do it. What aren't you going to speak about next?

She swayed slightly, a flower in the wind, and clung to the back of a chair, as if she were spent, before she raised her head and gave the title.

" 'An Old Woman Dies in Time of War.' "

Uncle Johnnie got up and went out, walking on several outraged ladies. Fumbling for his hat, he could hear Christabel's voice,

"Sorrow on sorrow, a shadow that falls in the night——"

The butler, who had retired for a few words with the waiters in the dining room, got to the front door just too late. It closed with a bang loud enough to make all the adoring ladies jump.

Chapter Sixteen

WHEN the war was over, Christabel went back to her writing. While she was at work on her whimsical romance, *O Fair Dove*, Uncle Johnnie had heard her say—not to himself, "It will be ignored and hated."

"Oh no! Why, I'm sure it will be a great success!" a voice had answered, whose voice he didn't remember, for Eliza's drawing room had been full that afternoon, and Mrs. Russell had distracted his attention by talking to him.

"I've tried bone-meal around the roots, and I've tried soot——" Mrs. Russell said, and through her voice Christabel's voice had replied:

"I write for the few—I can say this to you, because I do feel that you are an understanding person—and if there is even one who hears what I'm saying, that will be all I ask."

I hear what you're saying, thought Uncle Johnnie. "—whale-oil soap," said Mrs. Russell. "But of course, if they've already begun to curl up ——"

"I do *indeed* understand," the understanding person answered, earnestly. "One feels that in all your work there is that quality of truth too deeply and sensitively felt to be easily understood ——"

"Every *one* of them with the yellows!" Mrs. Russell said, triumphantly, in a duet with Christabel's:

"If it is a success—what the world calls a success—that will mean to me that it is an utter failure."

So when *O Fair Dove* turned out to be a best seller, he wondered what Christabel would say. He never doubted her ability, but he was curious.

Calling on Susannah one afternoon, he voiced his curiosity.

"If thee really wants to know, I have a letter from the dear child that came this morning." She left the room to get it, and Uncle Johnnie sat looking at a small table on which bronze elephants held between them *Stars and Wild Strawberries*, by Christabel Caine, *Carnation Flower*, by Christabel Caine, *Rocket Fire: Poems of War*, by Christabel Caine, *Fly in Amber*, by Christabel Caine, *O Fair Dove*, by Christabel Caine. A bowl of sweet peas stood before a large photograph of Christabel letting off bubbles of silvery light, as a fish in an aquarium lets off bubbles of air. A grand picture, Uncle Johnnie thought. But I fear you'll never be a really great whimsical writer, because you can't very well be photographed smoking a pipe.

Susannah returned. "This is the part—hmm—let me see—yes, here: 'Thank you for your congratulations, dearest. Yes, it *is* exciting—we never dreamed of anything like this when you were starting me on my 'literary career,' did we? I hope my head won't be turned with all the lovely things you and all the rest of my kind, kind friends, known and unknown, are saying to me. It *does* make me proud, but at the same time it makes me very humble, and it teaches me all over again that when one gives one's best, simply and from the heart, resisting all temptation to try to make an effect, one touches something universal. It does give one faith in one's fellow creatures, that swift generous response.' "

She put the letter between elephant and sweet peas, sat up straighter than ever, folded her hands above her belt, and looked at her brother over her spectacles.

"There, Johnnie! I think that answers thy question!"

Irma Goff waited, sitting on the edge of an old red velvet chair, her feet crossed in an easy position, her fingers clutching her bag until they ached. She was going to interview Christabel Caine; her first important interview, and she wouldn't have been given it to do if Bess McCleary, chosen first, hadn't ordered crab salad for lunch yesterday. Oh, make me able to do it all right, she prayed silently. Please, please make it all right.

222

The room was as cold and still as the grave. Clearing her throat sounded loud.

"Mrs. Carey will see you in her sitting-room, madam."

She followed the butler into the lift, and seeing herself in the mirror, tried to put on an expression of indifference, even scorn. If only her knees would stop shaking——

Please make it all right——

A tea-table with a lace cloth was drawn before the fireplace. The butler lit the fire, drew the curtains, hiding the streaming rain, and left her. My, this is cozy, she said to herself, unconvincingly.

She waited, sunk in a chair so deep and low she felt as if she were lying on the floor. At first she was motionless, listening, not only with her ears, but with her whole body. But presently she began to look about. Would it be all right to snoop a little? She struggled up out of her chair.

Sea-green and ash-pink chintz, a carpet with

faded sheaves of wheat and wreaths of flowers.
She took out her notebook and wrote:

"Aubosson—Aubuson—Aubousson—Aubus-
son—???—carpet."

Two corner cabinets held jade trees, with red
coral fruits and moon-white mother-of-pearl
blossoms, widespread or in cuplike bud.
"Chinese cabinets speaking of junk-filled seas,"
she wrote, and, thinking, I want to make it
kind of quaint, like her own writing, added,
"Every soft chair seemed to say, do sit in my
lap."

Violets all round, bowlfuls! Irma was used
to a bunch of them, with stems in green foil
and an edging of those other leaves, the hard
shiny ones that kept, not masses like these,
bowls and bowls of them.

Some books on a low table. *O Fair Dove*,
bound in green morocco; the English edition of
Fly in Amber; Fleur d'Oeillet, par Christabel
Caine——*Bells of the Temple*, by Geoffrey
Strade. She opened that one. Young Mr.
Strade looked at her sternly from the frontis-

piece, in his shirt—mercy, how decla*tay*, thought Irma—and with something behind his ear, hollyhock or hibiscus flower. There was a dedication, "To Christabel Caine," and on the fly-leaf, in blackest ink, "C. C. from G. S., to say all the things that can never be said." It had been written so violently that the pen had ploughed through the paper in the stroke beneath the words.

She was looking at it when a voice said: "How kind of you to come to see me," making her heart nearly jump out of her mouth.

She had felt that she looked so nice, in her Alice-blue sports suit, with an Alice-blue hat trimmed with sand-color, sand-colored shoes and stockings, and just a touch of the new orange rouge Bess McCleary was so crazy about. But now, looking at Christabel Caine, in simple filmy black, with pearls, she felt too light, too obvious.

"What a dreadful day! You're very brave to venture out. Come closer to the fire. An

225

open fire is such a friendly thing, don't you think?"

"I *certainly do*!"

"Fire and flowers and books, and a room is furnished—for me! But I have a fear of becoming possessed by possessions that I'm afraid I carry to extremes. Cream or lemon? Though you really shouldn't take either with this jasmine tea."

"Over our steaming cups of jasmine tea," Irma wrote in her mind. The lacquer cup was so unexpectedly light that she nearly dashed the tea into her face.

Marvelous sandwiches, caviare. Miss Caine —Mrs. Carey—which ought she to say?—took one on her plate, but didn't eat it, and didn't pass them again to Irma, who wanted another awfully. She didn't often get a chance at caviare, and there were other kinds that looked exciting, too. Besides, she had only had time for an ice-cream soda for lunch. She tried saying in her mind, "*Might* I have another of those very delicious sandwiches?" There they

226

were, and, after all, why shouldn't she? But somehow she didn't. It would have looked so greedy, with Miss Caine not touching hers.

She had a sudden vision of mamma and Velma and herself making sandwiches in the kitchen back home, trying new kinds out of the women's magazines, sometimes grandly buying a little yellow pot of *foie gras*, when mamma was going to have the Just Sew Club, or the bunch was coming to play bridge. When they were passed everyone would say, "Mmm! how yummy!" or, "Oh, now, listen, Mrs. Goff! I've had *nine!*" and mamma would answer: "Go on, take some! There's nothing to them!" She felt suddenly weak with homesickness.

I guess I ought to begin interviewing. Oh, dear! How do I begin? Oh, please let me know how to do it all right! *Please!*

But with a gush of gratitude she realized that the interview had begun.

"I have a ridiculous terror of being interviewed," Christabel Caine was saying, her voice low, yet so clear that each word stood by itself, exquisite and apart as if it were inclosed in a glass bell. "You must be kind to me. Because—it sounds absurd, I know—I'm very shy. I think perhaps it comes from my lonely childhood. I must have been a funny little person, growing up alone, in a big old house with a big old garden, talking to the flowers and the butterflies."

"Oh, that's lovely! *Do* you mind if I take notes? You see, this is my very first important interview——"

"Really!"

"You see, I thought newspaper work would be the best training I could get, because I kind of—I guess you certainly must get tired of people saying—I hope to write."

"Really! Have you done anything yet?"

"Well, I did some poems—verses, I guess I *should* say—that some magazines took, and I want to do enough for a book. I wanted to do a series of Western wildflower poems—my home's in Colorado. Spanish bayonet and Indian paintbrush. The one I'm really dying to do is Mariposa lily ——"

"Mariposa lily?"

"M-mariposa's Spanish for butterfly—well, I guess you know that better than I do! White, with sort of faint lilac streaks—it's p-perfectly lovely. It's sort of hard to—it grows up in the m-mountains ——"

What's the *matter* with me, stammering this way?—she wailed to herself. But the thought of the luminous lilac-veined petals comforted her.

"I see. Flowers mean a great deal to you, just as they do to me. I've tried to express my love for them in some of my poems."

"Oh, I know! 'White lilac, delicate and cool,' and 'Heather in the mist,' and the one about the scarlet tulip being like the Holy Grail!"

"Those among others. I always have been passionately attached to 'green things growing.' I remember when I was tiny there was an old thousand-leafed rose-bush I used to tell my troubles to."

"Lonely kiddie tells trouble to roses," Irma's pencil flew.

"Before I could write, I used to make up little stories and tell them to the beetles and the hoptoads in the garden. There has been a good deal of loneliness in my life, as it happens, and I hope that it has made me a little more understanding of the loneliness of others. I have always tried so hard never to let the heartaches that have come my way make me sorry for myself. I have tried to turn them into pity and understanding. One wants so terribly just to try to help the hurts a little—not to let suffering make one hard."

"Have you a literary creed, Miss Caine?"

"I believe in truth. I think I could say that is not only my literary creed, but the creed I try to live by. Truth, crystal-clear, like cold water. What if it hurts? I believe in the diamond-hardness of truth. Softness is the end of everything."

230

"Truth—hard—c. water—wh if hurts?" Irma wrote under the note that said "Pity and u-standing. Don't let suff make hard," twisting her head a little, trying to ease the pain in the back of her neck.

"Now, what I have tried to do in *O Fair Dove* ——"

"Well, I mustn't trespass on your kindness any longer," Irma said at length. "I just don't know *how* to thank you!"

"Thank *you*, with all my heart! *Good*-by, Miss—uh—. Smedley will show you out."

But Irma had to turn back again to cry:

"Oh, you just can't know how much you mean to people!"

Christabel absent-mindedly ate several sandwiches after Miss Goff left. Generally she disliked being interviewed by women, and certainly it was strange, to put it mildly, of the paper to send a novice. But the little thing had been rather touching, she thought, popping a whole sandwich into her mouth, and she was glad she had given her such a good time. How naïve she had been in her surprise at finding a celebrity so human!

The mild glow faded, boredom and restlessness crept over her. She roamed about the room, picking up a book, putting it down, shaking the sofa pillows into shape, stretching out her arms and yawning, yawns that ended in moans. She was sick and tired of this room and everything in it, the wishy-washy chintz, Marie Laurencin's gray-faced ladies with their small strawberry-ice-cream pink mouths matching their strawberry-ice-cream pink ribbons, the "amusing" shell flowers—*amusing!* Evelyn Thompson had done the decorating for her. She liked helping poor Evelyn, who had had hard times since her divorce. She had given her work, and sent little Roberta to the twins' dancing class. But the room had never expressed her real self. Marvin Marcy-Jones was going to do it over for her. There was a square of purple carpet, to try, on the floor,

232

and lengths of orange stuff trailed on to it, from a chair. Evelyn's feelings would be hurt, and she herself probably wouldn't like it any better. Still, Marvin felt that he really had caught her personality. Perhaps he had. Perhaps it would be all right.

Oh, *what* do I want to do? Shall I call up Marvin? She drifted to the telephone, pausing to write on the pad beside it, "Mariposa lilies." Standing tapping her cheek with the pencil, she decided she didn't want to see Marvin. Elliott? Austin? Gobby?

She picked up the telephone and gave a number.

"Is Count du Sanglier there? . . . Thank you. . . . Mrs. Carey." Then: "Maurice, this is Christabel. Oh, you nice person! I needed that!"

She felt her twittering nerves grow still, her whole being relaxed to velvet smoothness, velvet softness.

"Maurice, take pity on me! If I don't put on a flame-colored frock with no back and go

233

somewhere to dance tonight I shall die—and Curtis is in Washington. Somewhere with very loud jazz and cocktails in coffee-cups ——"

Listening to his answer, she sank into a low chair, smiling a little, shutting her eyes.

"Don't be silly ——! . . . I'll tell you when I see you—maybe! . . . *Au 'voir* ——"

Putting the receiver into its hook, she lay with the telephone against her breast, in a silence that still vibrated with Maurice's words.

When she finished writing her interview that night Irma Goff was still too excited to sleep, in spite of the hour. So she wrote to mamma and Velma, telling them all about it.

"The most marvelous house! First I was shown in by the butler—ahem!—while I attempted to give a correct imitation of Mrs. Astorbilt, and I think I fooled him, into this wonderful drawing-room all red velvet that looked about a million years old. Mamma, I bet you would think the chairs needed recovering, but they looked like things right out of

234

the Metropolitan Museum. But I didn't interview her there, but in front of the open fire in her own boudoir, wasn't that sweet of her, just like I was one of her intimate friends, a simply *darling* room, with heaps of violets absolutely everywhere and the most *marveelious* tea, caviare sandwiches 'n' everything. Well, Mamma and Velma, you can imagine the thrill of meeting CHRISTABEL CAINE, though you can bet I didn't let her see how excited I was. I was kind of scared, too, but as it turned out, I needn't have been, because after we got friendly she confessed that she was very shy and actually had been scared of *me*—could you believe it?

"I kept thinking about Mrs. Coffy's paper on her at the Club last winter, and what she'd think if she could see me! She's simply *beautiful*, very young-looking in spite of having two adorable twin kiddies, 5 yrs. old, but kind of sad-looking and quiet, and all in black. I wonder if she's in mourning for anyone? I didn't like to ask—I kept feeling as if she'd had some terrible sorrow sometime and that's what makes her work so wonderful. It wasn't her husband, because she spoke simply marvelously of him and what a help his interest was to her in her work. She was wonderful about my writing, *really* interested. It's made me crazy to do something worth while. When I was going I said 'I'm going to try to write harder than I ever have in my life, this very evening!' and she said 'Do you know, so am I!' It sort of thrills me to think of her sitting there all alone writing. She told me some nights she works *all night long!*

"Just as I was going she picked up an enormous bunch of the violets out of one of the bowls and gave them to me. I have them here on my desk, in front of a great big signed photograph she gave me!!!"

Chapter Seventeen

O<small>N A</small> March morning, as every morning, Minnie pulled back the blue silk curtains, closed the windows, lit the fire, and turned on the bath water. Wakened by gentle noises, Christabel stretched, yawned, put her white feet into blue mules held by kneeling Minnie, wrapped herself in blue silk embroidered with daisies bigger than her head, and trailed to the bathroom.

Steam fragrant with perfume created to express her personality veiled black men peeping from behind orchid-dripping trees, painted on her bathroom walls by young Boris Orlovski, a cousin of the Czar's, some people thought. She was wonderful to exiled Russians. "More wonderful to the men than the women," catty Mrs. Wickett said, but this Christabel felt was not worth noticing, it was so evidently caused by jealousy.

"It's rather amusing how ladies give themselves away!" she had said to Gobby, when he indignantly reported Mrs. Wickett's remark. "I did my best to make Boris and one or two others be nice to Adéle Wickett when they were all here one afternoon, and they were just as naughty as they could be." She laughed tolerantly. "Poor Adéle! Naturally she consoles herself by blaming me!"

Besides, she had had several little Russian countesses in national costume sing at her teas.

After her bath came her breakfast tray, heaped with mail. Advertisements and appeals had been suppressed by Ellen Beach, her adoring young secretary, granddaughter of the distant cousin who had jilted Uncle Johnnie. The photographs of crippled children made her feel too badly, and, after all, one could do so little. Of course big checks went to really deserving charities, but Curtis took care of that. Indiscriminate giving was apt to do more harm than good, was really just self-indulgence.

Invitations, letters from strangers:

238

"Dear Miss Caine:

"May a lonely shut-in thank you for having helped her pass weary wakey hours when other folks were fast asleep ———"

"Mrs. Christabel Caine:
"Dear Madam:

"I am a Junior in High School. I have been given you as a subject for an essay, and would be obliged if you would tell me some facts about yourself that would be of interest, also what caused you to write each of your books and something about what you have wished to express in them, and anything else you can think of ———"

"Dear Christabel Caine (For a Dear you are and ever will be, for writing your Beautiful Books)

"I'm not quite a stranger, for although *you've* never heard of *me*, I know *you* intimately, and I've chuckled with you and I've wept with you (Yes, truly!) and in all my life nothing, except feeling the wind blow through my hair in a sailboat, and stealing (don't look so shocked!) a sprig of lavender, sun-kissed and bee-beset, from Ann Hathaway's garden, has given me quite the same sort of utterly joyous delight your books have ——"

From the clipping bureau came best-seller lists. *O Fair Dove. O Fair Dove. O Fair Dove.* Reviews. She read:

"Its lovely pages glow with a sort of luminous tenderness, a 'light that never was, on sea or land.'"

"If more novels like *O Fair Dove* came to the critic's table, how much happier life would be! Written with exquisite sensitiveness and poignant beauty, this whimsical romance demands the use of the important word genius ——"

So buoyant, she felt she hardly touched the pillow. Drinking the delicious hot coffee, she dreamily reread "exquisite sensitiveness—poignant beauty—genius—" When Curtis looked in to say good morning and good-by she returned his kiss warmly.

"Good-by, darlingest! Isn't it a day straight from *heaven?*" She kissed her finger-tips, fluttered them toward the door, and, still smiling, drew out the next clipping.

"Ever since women discovered that novel-writing is infinitely preferable to housekeeping, and much less exacting, they have written innumerable stories. *O Fair Dove*, by Christabel Caine, is just another of them. The story, buried under would-be whimsicality, is ordinary, the characters are puppets, and the ending is a relief. The exhausted reader may well wonder whether he or the authoress has wasted the more time."

There was a pain in her chest. How could people be so unkind? How could even jealousy make them so cruel? She was terribly, terribly hurt. Not that she minded honest criticism, she *welcomed* it, but this was wanton abuse. With hands that shook she tore the clipping into tiny pieces—tiny ——

The twins came tearing in, flinging their arms around her, scrambling up on the bed. She put her hands over her ears.

"Gently, darlings! Mother doesn't feel very well this morning. *Marigold!* Be careful of that tray! Now go to Mademoiselle at once, both of you!"

With the match that lit her cigarette she touched the torn clipping on the ash tray. It writhed and turned to ash. "——luminous tenderness——" she read again. "——genius ——." "Some more reviews for you to paste in," she said, handing them to Ellen Beach, who came in with her engagement book.

"May I read them? Oh, what nice ones! Isn't it marvelous, there hasn't been a single unfavorable review of *O Fair Dove*, has there? Not that there ought to be, only it's so wonderful that people really appreciate it."

"What do I have to do today, Ellen? Luncheon at Pierre's, Ivan Korovine's class, tea with Austin Weeks, and the Treasure

242

Seekers here for dinner. I'll see Mrs. Briton about dinner now."

"Mrs. Caine's train gets in at four."

"Oh, Ellen, *no!* Is it *today* mother's coming? Well, send the big car for her, and tell her I'm *heart*broken and I'll be back just as early as I *possibly* can. That makes it awfully awkward about dinner ——"

"I needn't come ——"

"Ellen, don't be silly! With your young man coming? No, I'll manage somehow. Mother may be too tired to want to come down, anyway."

Mrs. Britton entered. Spring lamb, green peas. The telephone rang. Ellen asked over her shoulder if Mrs. Carey would see some one from the *World?* Minnie asked, which dress? Asparagus, perhaps, instead of a salad. The telephone rang. Would Mr. and Mrs. Carey dine with Mrs. Wickett next Thursday, with bridge afterward? Beige dress, Minnie, and the dark brown hat. Strawberry mousse in a

243

spun sugar basket. Mrs. Carey is ex*treme*ly sorry ——

She was ready to go out at last, in the red-and-black car, so small, so smart, looking as if one wound it up with a key, with Bates seeming so a part of it that one almost expected to see a tiny crack running down his front, splitting a black tin cap and a pink tin nose, one felt that an iron tail must run into a hole in the seat, to keep him steady.

Buying her own books, she thought, how excited this little person would be if he knew I was the author! She felt like a queen incognito.

"Did I understand you to say *twelve* copies of *O Fair Dove?* Is that correct?"

And she answered, graciously, laughingly:

"Alas, yes! That's the penalty of writing a book, so many people expect the poor author to give them copies!"

His eyes and his mouth were three round O's, she thought, walking up Fifth Avenue, amused and touched. Well, that was a real thrill in

his dull day. She could hear him telling the
other clerks: "That was Christabel Caine!
That lady I was just waiting on!"

The day was so lovely that she had sent the
car away. Turning down a side street, she
went into the Catholic church where she liked
to say her prayers or meditate. Sometimes she
longed to be a Catholic. If only she could stop
thinking, how restful it would be.

Beyond the rood screen lights wavered in
white and blue cups, banked into shapes of
hearts and crosses, on either side of the altar,
where a nun knelt, rose to dust the vases of
artificial lilies, knelt again. All work should
be done that way, with love and prayer, Christabel thought. Other nuns knelt motionless.
She was kneeling with them. She was kneeling
alone, the bride of Christ, lost in ecstasy, while
out in the church, heartbroken, adoring, knelt
Elliott and Maurice and the new poet who was
coming to dinner tonight. She almost added
Curtis, but the thought of him floated out
without embodying.

Oh, to be there, safe and at peace, free of earthly possessions, free of selfhood, wrapped in love forever!

But out on the Avenue again, she knew that God wanted His children to be happy and free in His sunshine! Everything was holy, if you had eyes to see. She looked with seeing eyes at a top-shaped female in black satin, at a taxi that came squealing to the curb in answer to her look, at her florist's window.

"Good *morn*ing, Mr. Johnson. . . . Yes, indeed, divine! Quantities of flowers, please— mimosa for the drawing room, I think—you know how much I need. I'm just going to be banal and have a few tulips for the library, those flame-colored ones and a few mauve. . . . Oh, I don't know, three or four dozen. Now *what* have you, really intriguing, for the dinner table? I'm using the ruby glass tonight. . . . Not, not a very big dinner, twenty people, and not a bit the roses-silver-pheasants type ——"

What a difference it makes, being human with people, she thought, as Mr. Johnson flung

246

himself into originality, bringing flowers like lobster claws for her inspection, flowers like strings of doll's china eyes, as he presented her with a spray of jasmine to wear.

She turned back, as she was leaving, to order a big purple basket of double and single violets for the Glenworthy girls, Clothilde, Eugénie, Ellaline, poor old maids, relics of her mother's girlhood. They adored her, and she had seen their letters to her mother, telling of all the wonderful things she had done for them. She did try to be thoughtful. When she had them to tea she was never at home to other callers, for she told herself they wouldn't want to meet anyone, they were so shabby, coming in scarecrow finery, always bringing some pathetic present. Last time, half a dozen drying daffodils with lots of asparagus fern, lost in her roomful of flowers. "We tried to get Mariposa lilies because of that lovely poem of yours your dear mother very kindly sent us, but the florists didn't seem to know what they were." She had been so touched, and had filled their

247

arms from the drawing-room vases when they went. She loved to heap gifts on them, poor old things—an armful of novels, a nearly full box of *marrons glacés*. That last time, Elliott had called up to ask if he might come to tea, and she had had to hustle them off. She had been meaning to do something nice to make up. She would ask them to dinner, tomorrow, with mother, just a nice intimate time, with no one else, and then they would all go to the Racine revival that Countess du Sanglier had arranged and that Mrs. Towne had sent her tickets for. That would be a real thrill for them, and it would be a delight to hear some pure French. She wrote on her card, to go with the violets, "Will you dine and go to the theater tomorrow? I'll send the motor at seven. Most affectionately, C. C. C."

Why did so few people realize that the only sure way of being happy was to make others happy?

It was a day for a new hat. Everyone in the shop swam at her.

"Isn't that peculiar, Mrs. Carey, Miss M'ree was just this morning speaking of you, wasn't she, girls? We have some lovely things to show you—Gladys, bring that Maria Guy with the banana ribbon—and listen, dear, the blue ballibuntl, you know, the one with the choux over the ear, and, honey! Listen! Tell Miss M'ree Mrs. Carey's here, I know she'll want to see her."

Marie herself appeared. "*Misss-us* Carey, good morning! No, no, no! Take these away. Bring me the little black horsehair with the nose veil that hasn't been shown yet."

"Oh, adorable!"

"Doesn't moddom look adorable?"

"A work of art," Marie pronounced.

"A picture!"

"It looks just like moddom, doesn't it?"

That was in an undertone, for her to overhear. She was on to their ways! But it did, it was a divine hat.

"I must take it with me! I *must* wear it out to lunch. Will you call me a taxi, please?"

Waiting for it, she remembered to ask about Miss Lola's headaches, Miss Vera's sister, who used to be in the shop before her marriage. "What a memory!" they exclaimed, pleased and flattered, and through their exclamations she heard Miss Pearl saying to another customer, just audibly:

"Christabel Caine, who wrote *O Fair Dove*."

Alfred was scurrying into her sitting room with orange tulips. She had caught the servants by surprise, for she had said she wouldn't be in until after lunch. But she was human with him, too; she saw his face relax a little as he went to get her a cocktail.

A press photographer took her picture as she entered Pierre's, a careful ten minutes late. Maurice kissed her hand and noticed her hat, the head waiter had a charmed murmur as he led them to their table, friends saluted as they passed.

"Come to a movie after lunch. There's a new one with the intriguing Charlot."

"Alas! I have to go on to my class. Ivan

Korovine, you know, the Russian who had something to do with—with—I can't remember his name for the moment, the one who had that place in France. He teaches you to free yourself through color and rhythm, and he has simply marvelous ideas about sex sublimation."

"Ah, little grown-up girl! You think you are too old for a doll, so you play with your soul!"

"*Play*, Maurice! It isn't play, it's intense concentrated work. I come away *limp*. But it makes life seem a very different thing. I don't think I ever before this year, *fully* realized its intensity and re*al*ity."

"Come to the movies. Movies and jazz and burlesque queens and—what else? Vermilion and magenta—seem to me as real intensities as you'll find in a rather vague world."

"Well, of course, everyone admits that Charlie Chaplin is our one great tragedian. But——"

"If you don't, you will be sorry tomorrow, when I am to be very ill."

Through the new nose veil she made round questioning eyes.

"Certainly. Haven't you heard that *maman* is *patronne* for an evening of Racine?"

"And you, too, dread it?"

"No, I simply avoid it."

"*Moi aussi!*"

Mademoiselle could go with mother and the Glenworthy girls. It would be a glimpse of heaven for her and she could translate anything they couldn't understand.

"So come to the movies!"

She yielded, laughing. "But I must be through in time to get down to a studio on Ninth Street for tea. A man is doing a portrait of my precious twinnies that I promised to come and criticize. Oh, Maurice, I really dread it! I can't tell you why—yes, I think I will, after all! You see, I'm terribly afraid he's in love with me, poor darling—I can tell you this, you being you, without being afraid that you'll think I'm conceited, it's simply that it's such a problem, I *don't* know what to do, and I need advice. Do you think you could put yourself in the position of a gentleman laid low by my fatal charm?"

"*C'est moi.*"

"You see, he's such a sensitive person that if I'm horrid to him, as I suppose I should be, he might do *any*thing, and if I'm kind to him, that's even worse! I want to help him, and I don't know what to do. It makes me *triste à pleurer!* I only tell you because it's rather an interesting situation psychologically, and because you'll never know who the man is."

"Don't begin to worry about the men who love you, or you'll have time for nothing else."

"Oh, Maurice! *Flatteur!*" She smiled, delicately self-mocking. But her heart gave a skip. I've never seen him look so—so as if he were holding something in. Oh, my poor Maurice! not you, too? And aloud she cried, in a voice that annoyed her by sounding fluttered:

"Oh, I *don't* think any pastry! Well—one of those strawberry tarts, because it's spring,

253

and if I can't eat any tea I shall tell Austin Weeks you're to blame."

When Curtis came home from the office there was either silence, that meant Christabel was out, or the twitter of voices as he passed the library door on the way to his room. And although he vaguely knew that the voices were settling things, beauty, truth, real art, immortality, sex in its relation to this or that, and the meaning of life, it never occurred to him that it could matter whether or not the sound remained twitter or was resolved into words. Sometimes Christabel called him in, tipping a cheek to his polite kiss, clinging to him with a white hand, asking, "Darling, some tea?" Sometimes she allowed him to tiptoe upstairs to relax on his sofa with the market quotations and a highball.

This evening there was silence. He caught a glimpse of Smedley arranging a centerpiece, launching himself across so big a table that Curtis knew Christabel and he must be giving a dinner. He would have liked to see his children, but it annoyed Nurse to have him come in at supper-time. She said it made them show off, sticking out their lips at their lovely cereal, and jumping about, and later Michael, who was easily excited, was apt to imagine lions under the bed. And Christabel supported her.

No sign of Christabel. Out with an affinity, probably. I believe I'll get an affinity, myself. Adèle Wickett? She's pretty, even if Christabel doesn't think so, and she nearly dies laughing when I tell her a joke. Or Helen Vanessi, with her black hair low on her white neck, and those eyes—oh, boy! She likes me, too, he thought.

Well, he would just have a look at the stock quotations. Dropping down on his sofa with a sigh, the paper slid from his hand. I am very, very tired, he thought. A hard day. Donelly says he can get me three cases of the real pre-war stuff. A very hard day. That lobster at lunch was certainly nice and tender ——

He yawned, arching his back, stretching out his arms, grasping air.

Poor old Harry.   I'll never see *that* money again ——

Keep my left arm straight—left arm straight —a white ball ran across a stretch of green and trickled into the cup.   Ought to get dressed— very very tired—very very very tired——

Chapter Eighteen

THE porter made Mrs. Caine trot to keep up with him. Between the way he hurried and the people who pushed between them, she had hard work keeping her eye on her bag, with her silver brush and mirror in it, and her aquamarine brooch set in seed pearls. But when he asked, "Taxi?" over his shoulder, and she answered with quiet dignity, "I think a private car will meet me," his manner changed entirely. And when he saw the big Rolls-Royce, with chauffeur and footman, he became so polite that she had to add another quarter to the quarter she had clutched, ready, ever since she got off the train.

She sat up very straight, looking at her reflection in the front window, made into a mirror by the two impressive plum-covered backs. She felt shy and conspicuous. But she scolded herself. Don't be so silly! Nobody's looking at you! Relax! She relaxed firmly.

The house was full of flowers. "Well, you look very festive, Smedley," she said, giving the butler the bunch of early daffodils from the garden she had brought for Christabel.

"Yes, madam. We're having a dinner to-night."

A dinner! Oh, dear, she thought, there'll be a lot of celebrities who won't want to talk to *me*. I wish to *good*ness there wasn't going to be a dinner!

Thank Heaven, she had made over her black evening dress, after a picture in *Vogue*. Fred said it looked fine. And, telling herself that no one would look at *her*, she was exhilarated by the thought that ran beneath—it does look nice!

It was late when Christabel rushed in, her cheeks glowing pink, her eyes starry.

"Oh, mother, mother, *moth*er! Oh, *dar*ling, how heavenly to have you! I was heart*bro*ken that I couldn't meet you! Did they tell you? It was just one of those things—*oooh!*"

"You're crushing—your—lovely gardenias,

258

dearie!" Mrs. Caine protested, her mouth full of fragrant fur. Christabel released her and held her at arm's length.

"Let me look at you. Oh, mother darling, you've gotten thinner! That's naughty of you. And you look *so* tired, dear."

"I'm not a bit ——"

"You're going to have a real rest while you're here. First, you're going to have a delicious hot bath with geranium salts, and then a nice little dinner on a tray, here in front of the fire. I wish I could have it with you, just us two, but, alas! we've got some stupid people dining here. I dread the thought! I won't inflict anyone on you tonight, darling, but tomorrow, when you're all rested, I've planned a little dinner, especially for you, and a theater party."

"Christabel, I really don't feel a bit tired ——"

"I don't believe you ever think about yourself long enough to know whether you feel tired or not, but now you have some one to think

259

about you in spite of yourself. How's my darling daddy?"

"Very well, and sent heaps of love. But Uncle Johnnie's been quite ill."

"Oh, too bad!"

"They think he may have to come———"

"Heavens! Look at the time! There's nothing I'd love better than to sit down and have a nice long talk, darling, and hear all the news, but if I don't *fly* ———!"

"Christabel! Who's coming to dinner tomorrow?" Mrs. Caine called after her, and she called back:

"The Glenworthy girls! Won't that be nice?"

Mrs. Caine went and had a long look at her evening dress, on its padded hanger. She saw herself coming down the broad stairs. "My mother———" "My mother———" She turned graciously from celebrity to celebrity, surprising them by her intelligence, her unaffected charm. Then she made a face, saying "The *Glen*worthy girls!" under her breath.

260

But, taking her bath, wrapping herself in a heated towel soft as deep moss, she saw herself against a background of old oak paneling, hothouse roses, Smedley's shirt front, fragile in filmy black, being gracious to the poor old Glenworthys.

"Christabel spoils me so. She thinks nothing is too good for her mother! And she worries about me ridiculously. Why, last night ——"

She got into the orchid bed-jacket Christabel had given her long ago. It was as nice as ever, for she only used it on her visits here. It almost hadn't been worn at all.

Nice Bessie, who never made her feel shy, as Smedley and Alfred and Minnie did, brought in her tray, and she said, graciously: "Well, Bessie! How have *you* been?" Dinner was delicious. Christabel had even remembered how she loved grapefruit. And there was a cluster of her favorite violets on the tray. Who but Christabel would think of a thing like that?"

Hearing gentle snores, Christabel sighed, smiled, and went in to wake Curtis with a kiss. "Darling, you must get *dressed!* It's almost dinner-time."

"Aw-w-igh——" he agreed through a yawn. "Who's coming tonight?"

"The Treasure Seekers."

"Oh, Gosh! *That* lot!"

"What do you mean by that lot?"

"Oh, all showing off and being sensitive souls, and the men a lot of sissies."

"Curtis, you *hurt* me when you speak of my friends that way."

"And not a pretty woman in the lot."

She kissed his arm lightly. "But they're all so worth while. Now do hurry, dearest."

She hadn't decided what to wear. Now Minnie stood waiting, while Christabel looked at rows of dresses. There hung the silver-blue gown, with silver stars thick about the hem, from Laura Burke's shop. She had said to Laura, "I'll wear it and advertise the shop to everybody," and Laura had cried gratefully:

262

"You must take it for a tiny little present—please, *please*, Christabel!"

She wouldn't hear of that. It was nonsense, when Laura was so poor, though of course Christabel had always been kind to her. She had worn it one evening, crying: "See! I've walked through the Milky Way! I've gotten stars all over my skirt!" And everyone had admired her in it. But somehow there had been no opportunity to mention Laura's shop without simply dragging it in. And though she meant to pay for it, Laura never sent a bill, and she had too much on her mind to be expected to remember. She was sick of the wretched gown and everything to do with it, for really, Laura and Laura's things were just a little bit too queer and arty to be taken seriously.

Ellen Beach looked in for the seating plan of the table, and Christabel bundled the gown into her arms.

"A little present. Wear it tonight."

"Oh *Christ*abel! Oh, *thank* you! It's divine. Oh, but you're too good to me!"

263

"It's just the color of your eyes. Your Nick will fall in love deeper than ever," Christabel said. She had yielded to a generous impulse and invited Ellen's *fiancé*, Nicholas Portal, to dinner. She hoped he would be presentable. Ellen, who should have been down putting the place cards around, leaned in the doorway, silver-blue folds pouring from her crossed arms, looking lost and happy. "Wake up, Ellen darling, wake up!" Christabel called to her. "I really do believe the child's in love!"

Ellen threw her arms tight around Christabel's neck, hiding her face, whispering:

"I am—I am!"

A Venetian lady in trailing silver, Christabel went to Curtis's dressing room, and found him in his underclothes, practicing golf strokes.

"Really, Curtis! You *must* get dressed. It's a quarter to eight. Mother came, but she's too ——"

Curtis's eyes glazed; he settled himself on his feet; his joined hands slowly lifted, then

264

swished in an arc through the air. He kept his head down. He had made a glorious drive.

Christabel stood in hurt silence, supported on one side by a shadowy Maurice, who lifted her white hand and kissed it, on the other by a shadowy sympathetic Austin. Again Curtis bent in a slight bow, again his joined hands slowly lifted.

"Curtis, *real*ly!"

"It's all in keeping your left arm straight," he told her, dreamily.

"Please try to be ready to receive our guests," she said. Feeling utterly wasted, she went to say good night to Michael and Marigold.

"Oh, Mummy, Mummy, my darlingest Mummy! Read us a story!"

"Read us Uncle Wiggly in the paper!"

"Uncle *Wig*gly! Darlings! You know Mummy never reads you anything like that."

"Daddy does."

"You know Mummy only reads you things that are beautiful or true."

265

"Tell us about Krazy Kat and Ignatz Mouse!"

"Michael!"

"Well, Alfred does. Ignatz hits Krazy with a brick, and Krazy says Powie! *Powie!* Powie!"

"Oh, *Mummy!* Michael swore! He said Powie! Michael *Carey*, aren't you ashamed of yourself? Mummy! Mummy!"

"Marigold! Children! Don't shout so! Mummy hasn't time to tell you a story tonight. Now get under the covers, darlings, and think that your beds were once trees, covered with little dancing leaves that sometimes were golden with sunlight and sometimes were silver with moonlight. And what did they hold tenderly, all night through, in their brown arms?"

"Tree toads!"

"No, darling, nests, safe warm nests to hold sleepy baby birds, and that's what you two are, sleepy little birds safe in your nests in the trees. *Mich*ael! Stop that noise!"

"I'm a bird! I'm singing."

266

"Now Mummy must go. Good night, my babies."

"Don't go! Don't go, my sweet beautiful Mummy!" Marigold cried, flinging her arms around Christabel, rolling her eyes; and Michael copied her. "My sweet beautiful Mummy!"

"She isn't your Mummy, she's my Mummy!"

"Darlings, darlings! Do you really love poor Mummy so much?" Christabel kissed soft firm cheeks, silky tops of heads, the little hollows in the backs of their necks.

"Ooh, *Mum*my! You tickle!"

"I don't like them getting wild'm; then it takes forever before they get to sleep," Nurse said, disapprovingly.

"My beautiful *'dorable* Mummy! They won't be anyone at the dinner party as beautiful as my shiny Mummy!"

"They'll do anything to stay up a little longer," Nurse put in. I really don't like her, Christabel thought, on her way to her mother's room. It is time for Nurse to go. Mademoiselle is enough for the children now.

Mrs. Caine had just finished dinner and pushed the grapefruit skin back into round so the servants shouldn't know she had been greedy and squeezed, when Christabel came in, trailing silver.

"How lovely you look! But are they wearing *trains*, Christabel?" she asked, for the dress she had made over was far from having a train.

"I don't really know what *they're* wearing, darling. Is it so very important?"

"Aren't you feeling well?"

"Oh, well enough—no, I'm not! I feel —— Oh, it isn't anything."

"You do too much, dear. You never spare yourself."

"I *am* tired. And—oh—Curtis is being a little—difficult—this evening; he always is when I have my special friends. I have his old bankers and golfers and bridge-playing *pret*-ty *wom*-en"—— she wrinkled her nose—"a thou-

268

sand times, and then I have my own kind, the people who really amount to something, writers and painters and musicians, just *once*, and he can hardly live through it. Oh, well, I ought to be used to it by now, only I do so *long* for a little understanding, a little give and take."

"Why, Curtis adores you, Christabel."

"Yes, of course he does. It's a wise little mother, and a comforting one. I wish I could stay up here with you, just the two of us, cozily! I'll be thinking of you all evening. Now go to bed soon and have a lovely sleep. Good night, dearest."

But nobody comes to New York for a lovely sleep, Mrs. Caine thought, rebelliously. Besides, she didn't feel sleepy. If she had been at home, she and Fred would just be starting for a movie or settling down to a game of Russian Bank. What's Fred doing now? she wondered, feeling rather homesick.

She tried to find something to read. There was *O Fair Dove*, but she knew that nearly by heart. A book by someone named Santayana. Edith Sitwell's poems.

> At Easter when red lacquer buds sound far slow
> Quarter-tones for the old dead Mikado,
>
> Through avenues of lime-trees, where the wind
> Sounds like a chapeau chinois, shrill, unkind,—
>
> The Dowager Queen, a curling Korin wave
> That flows forever past a coral cave ——

Well, of course it was nice, but what did it mean? Unfortunately, she had finished *The Saturday Evening Post* on the train. She loved it, though when it was mentioned Christabel smiled and said she hadn't the least doubt it had splendid stories.

There was thick creamy paper in the desk, with the address in fat letters. She rather liked the idea of writing to some of her friends, Anna McHugh, or Hattie Nelson, just to impress them. "I am here with Christabel ——" But the green quill, when pulled from its tumbler of shot, proved to have no pen in it, and it wouldn't have helped if it had, as the green-jade inkwell was empty. I don't think I'd better ring and ask for pen and ink, she thought. Probably everyone's busy helping with the dinner party.

But she had a pencil in her bag, so she wrote a long letter to Fred about how sweet and thoughtful Christabel was being.

Chapter Nineteen

LONELINESS, loneliness, Christabel thought, going downstairs, her heavy silver train sliding from step to step with a flat slapping sound. Who cares whether I live or die? Curtis thinks of nothing but his golf, Ellen cares for no one but her Nick Portal, Michael and Marigold are shut away in the bright selfishness of childhood. Loneliness——

She paused before the mirror halfway down the stairs—not that she cared how she looked to anyone who was coming tonight. Her shining bronze hair lay close as feathers to her head, silver clung close to her ivory body. A statue made of bronze, ivory, and silver. I am beautiful, she thought, feeling cold and sad. And what difference does it make? She tried to comfort herself by repeating things that Maurice had said, and Austin. They brought no glow. No one will know how sad I am tonight, she thought, going into the drawing room, answering welcoming cries, giving a hand here, there, comforted by her sadness.

Her guests were all there, for, like royalty, she preferred to be the last to appear at her own parties. The Treasure Seekers. She had gathered them together in the first place, men and women whose preoccupation was to seek the treasures of beauty hidden away in the heart of life. Tonight she could see why Curtis and Smedley were unenthusiastic about them. Hair a little too long, and either dusty or oily, too many barbaric ear-rings and touches of batik. One man among them was startlingly good-looking, taller than the rest. His eyes met hers as she entered the room; she felt a tingling warmth flow through her. Then he looked away, and down. Ellen, in the starry gown, had joined him.

Ellen's Nick Portal. Christabel was conscious of him all through dinner, her voice, low and clear, called words clever and yet compassionate down the table, for him to hear, her hand lay, a spray of frosty fern across her silver

273

breast, for him to see. But Ellen wasn't giving him a chance to notice anyone but herself. "Nick! Nick!" she called him back, whenever his attention wandered. Didn't she realize how tiresome that became to a man?

Christabel was conscious of the two of them through everything; through talking to her beautiful East Indian with his white turban, gold clothes, and dark purple mantle edged with a tracery of dark dim gold; or to her Irish poet; through noticing that Gobby, as usual, wasn't knowing when to stop on the salted nuts; through avoiding Elliott's meaning glances—idiot!—through saying, "Movies, saxophones, and bright magenta, seem to me perhaps the *on*ly real things in a shadowy world," and hearing the expected, "What was that she said?" Something was making Ellen look radiant tonight—the blue gown, or, possibly, love. But certainly she was making a fool of herself, languishing all over him, gazing at him, obviously adoring. And he is graciously allowing himself to be adored, Christabel thought, but if I'm not mistaken he's getting just a little bit fed up.

He looked in her direction. She lifted a shoulder, letting silver slide from it, and turned her lovely head. In her imagination she could see her hair gleam in the light from the tall candles.

"I needn't ask if you arranged those blossoms," her poet was saying with his mouth full. "Some ladies let their servants do it, I'm told, but I look at these, and I look at you, and I know."

Smedley was at the other end of the table, filling Curtis's champagne glass. "I never can understand people who let the servants do it," Christabel said. "That seems to me like letting the servants say your prayers for you."

Because, she thought, I *did* come in and give them that one touch that makes all the difference.

She turned her head slowly back, letting her eyes rest indifferently on Nick Portal. His were turned toward Ellen.

She had told everybody that she might possibly—just possibly—be able to get her Irish poet to recite some of his poems after dinner, and she had a hard time to keep him from starting before she had drawn him out. A wee wizened man like a monkey, bent in the monkey's attitude just before the jerk of the chain makes it begin to dance, he stood there, chanting his poems in Gaelic, chanting away with his eyes shut.

The East Indian sang, too, translating for them.

"Sing on! The birds in the forest sing, nor care whether anyone hears them. The flowers in the woodland bloom, nor care that there is no one to inhale their fragrance. Give all of thyself, no matter if thou perish——"

Oh, that is true, Christabel thought, looking towards Nick Portal. That is true!

Sitting in the great Venetian chair in which she never crossed her knees, hearing, "Hush! What is she saying?" when she spoke, she imagined herself going across the room to him, coming to him like a breeze from the sea, after Ellen's cloying sweetness. He will not come to me because he has pride and humility, she told herself. And she really rose and went across the room and sat down beside him.

Elliott and Gobby and Marvin Marcy-Jones rose, too, and came with her. And Nick Portal, after a politely indifferent sentence or two, got up and walked away.

The rope of pearls in which Christabel's fingers had been twisted snapped, pearls showered to the floor. All her guests were on their knees, hunting them, except Ellen and Nick, who had disappeared.

Uncle Johnnie was in a private hospital in New York, and Ellen Beach was on her way to see him, for Christabel, who had meant to go, was again too busy.

No one seemed to know exactly what was the matter with him, himself least of all. He apparently took only the mildest interest in the affair. "The trouble with Uncle Johnnie is that he never will face facts," Christabel had said to Ellen. She had been wonderful about going to see him at first, but he had such a way of dropping off to sleep every time she went, that she had given it up, although she still sent him potted apple trees in frail bloom, and bowls of Mrs. Britton's calves' foot jelly. "Poor Uncle Johnnie, he's aged terribly," she told Ellen. "This pa*thet*ic way of falling asleep——!"

The first time Ellen had gone to see him, she had thought, I will try to make up to him a little for grandmother's having broken his heart long ago. All the way to the hospital she had imagined the poor old man thinking of her as his Little Dream Granddaughter—no, Little Dream Daughter, for he would still be young enough for that in a dream. But now she knew him, she had to imagine other things.

She imagined telling Nick about her visit to the hospital. My little Ellen, my little shining angel—how do you hide your white wings when you walk through the streets? Not that

Nick ever said things like that, but she hoped
he felt them.

She knew, for he had told her, that Nick
loved her more than any man had ever loved
any woman, and yet she wanted to do things
to make him love her even more—to make him
love her as much as she loved him. Nick—
Nick. She printed his smile, his head thrown
back, his eyes looking at her, on the sidewalk,
on the sky. Ellen, darling—Ellen, you are so
sweet—Ellen, I love you.

I mustn't think about Nick when I'm cross-
ing the street. It makes my knees tremble so.

If only he and Christabel would like each
other! That's the only thing that makes me
miserable, she thought, singing a song inside
herself.

"I try so hard to make Nick realize what a
marvelous person Christabel is," she told Uncle
Johnnie. "He's *aw*ful! I just have to work
to make him be nice to her!" She couldn't help
glowing, for it was usually Christabel who had
to do that. She had heard it over and over

279

again. She felt her mouth twitching into a smile, and said, firmly, "It makes me terribly unhappy."

"It seems to," said Uncle Johnnie.

"No, but it *real*ly does! What's the *mat*ter with Nick? When you think how wonderful she is, and yet she's so unspoiled! She treats us all as if we were just as wonderful!"

"She does still permit us to turn our backs when we leave the presence chamber."

Ellen was horrified, and yet he made her laugh. "Oh, you don't understand her, either," she said. But she couldn't help liking him.

I hate him, Christabel thought, going to her workroom after talking to Nick Portal. No, I don't, I don't waste that much emotion on him —it's simply that he bores me excruciatingly. Poor foolish little Ellen! What *does* she see in him?

He had come just after Christabel had sent Ellen to see Uncle Johnnie. Christabel, going through the hall, had heard him tell Smedley he would wait, and had asked him into the library, with what she now realized was mistaken kindness. From where they sat she had seen their reflections in the glass of the bookcase doors. His dark good looks, her delicate beauty, side by side, had made her catch her breath. Too bad such looks as his had nothing behind them. No response, not a spark, except when she had said what a sweet little thing Ellen was. He had bored her so that she ached all over.

I must pull myself together, she thought. I must not let his emptiness drain me. I must get to work.

But how futile it seems to go on offering my gift to a world so indifferent that in spite of all its praise it does not even see what I offer.

And yet, because I am an artist, I must go on. There is no rest for me, no comforting.

She felt a sudden longing to be with some one who really understood. She picked up the telephone.

Maurice du Sanglier was evidently out. The

unanswered burring went on until she put down the receiver. A squeaky Japanese voice answered for Marvin Marcy-Jones, "Not home, please!" Austin Weeks was broken-hearted, but was awaiting a fat female who was coming to beg him to paint her portrait. Elliott had no telephone.

Well, I really wanted to work, she thought, sitting down at her table, before the crystal that she always looked into first, to empty her mind of its tumult. Gazing at the tiny reflected Christabel, she bent her hot forehead to the cool smooth ball.

Stillness. Stillness. I am silent and empty. Well up within me, living water.

No ink in her fountain pen. Being in love was all very well, but Ellen was really getting inexcusable.

My work is the only thing that matters, she said to herself. Happiness, love, peace—I have relinquished them all for my work. I would go on writing if I knew no one would ever read a word that I had written.

282

Ellen, in her simplicity, had revealed that Nick had never read any of Christabel's books. Or was it simplicity?

I must get to work, Christabel thought.

There had been something in his eyes—a look of discontent. Perhaps already he was disillusioned, but too gallant a gentleman to let Ellen know. Perhaps that was the reason for his aloofness. When he had returned her dropped handkerchief, he had been careful not to let their fingers touch. He hardly looked at me, she thought. Was that the reason? What else? What other reason could there be?

Oh, if that is it, how *well* I understand, she told him in her mind. Happiness—loyalty— one makes one's choice.

She went to the mirror and looked deep into her own sad eyes. Child of sorrow, she thought, her fingers automatically pushing wings of bright hair forward. Then she rang for Alfred, who reported that Miss Beach had not yet returned and the gentleman was still waiting.

"Tea for two—no, for three, at once, in the library, Alfred," she said. "And whisky and soda. And if anyone else calls, I'm not at home."

Chapter Twenty

I wish Ellen and Nick would be married and get it over with, Christabel thought, turning her hot pillow, listening, to a distant clock strike three. I am sick of them both.

Curtis said Nick always acted as if he were giving the girls a treat, just by existing. She found balm in what he said; she resented it.

She pushed her hair up from her forehead; she turned over again. Her chest ached so that it was hard to breathe. Curtis is right, she thought. Nick is insufferably conceited. She saw in the dark the complacent corners of his beautiful mouth. Conceited, unintelligent, self-centered.

I have been pleasant to him all these weeks. I will go on being pleasant to him, simply because I am so indifferent to him that I can't admit him into the intimacy of rudeness.

She sat up in bed, turned on the light, and drank thirstily. She felt feverish and ill. That must be why she was so bored with everything and everybody—work, friends, Curtis, and the children. No one seemed real but Nick Portal, and she hated him.

Lying in the dark again, she thought incredulously that other people believed they were happy or unhappy, believed that what they were feeling mattered. She tried to call back feelings that had seemed intense once, before she knew Nick. Not even shadows answered. Yet he was everything she disliked, and she was filled with pity for Ellen, facing a lifetime with him. Nick and Ellen, together. "No!" she cried aloud, pressing her face into her pillow.

I won't think about him any more. He means nothing to me, except psychologically. As a person, he is a bore. As a study, he fascinates me, he amuses me.

He amuses me, she repeated to herself, and began to cry.

When the clock struck four, she got up,

washed her hot wet face, put on her dressing-gown, and wrote:

"My dear Nick Portal:

"Will you come to tea this afternoon, to talk over a business matter? My husband and I are most anxious to remodel the gardens of his old home in the country ———"

She finished the note, made changes, threw it away, and labored over another and another before she had one spontaneous enough to be copied out.

"Will you do something for me, darling?" she asked Curtis in the morning. "I long for a real country summer. *Would* you be willing to spend it on the Farm? I'm so sick of Southampton, and sitting on the sand in silk, with pearls and gloves. And Europe is worse —the Lido, and the horrible Lido young—well, men, I suppose. I've gone to these places for *you*, Curtis ———"

"Why, Christabel ———"

"Oh, I've gone gladly, dear. But this summer I'm not feeling very strong and I want to go back to quietness. I want to work a little in the garden, while the blessed babies tumble about underfoot and you practice putts into my flower-beds. I'm full of lovely plans. I'd even like to make a few little changes, if we could find just the right man. I'll have to think. You don't know how I've hungered and thirsted for the real country."

"Why, Christabel, I always liked the Farm, but I thought you didn't care anything about it."

"Curtis! Not care about the Farm? You *don't* know me very well, dearest, do you?"

"I'm so thankful! I really do believe Nick and Christabel are beginning to like each other," Ellen told Uncle Johnnie. "She agrees with him about lots of things that she never used to. It's awfully stimulating to listen to them. Of course they both have simply marvelous minds, and they argue like anything, and

288

then suddenly Christabel will say, 'You're right and I'm wrong,' with that sort of starry look she gets, that makes you want to kiss her. And I can tell she thinks what he says amounts to something, because sometimes she'll speak to him about something he's said, oh, three or four days before, and that she hasn't apparently paid any attention to at the time."

"He must find that flattering."

"Oh, he does. He thinks now she's quite intelligent. Imagine, that description for *Christabel*—quite intelligent!" She laughed with loving mockery.

"Christabel isn't usually so patient, if there's not a mutual attraction at once."

"Well, of course, everyone usually worships her right from the start—but then, so do they Nick. I couldn't understand either of them. But it's all right now, and the most marvelous thing is going to happen! Nick is going to do over the gardens at the Farm! It was Curtis who suggested having him, but I think it was Christabel who put it into his head, somehow, so that Nick and I could be together, because, of course, he'll have to be there a lot. In fact, I practically made her admit that was the reason. I really do think she's an angel!"

Christabel and Nick had motored out to the Farm, to plan the new gardens. New old lead figures against new old box, a square pool with water dripping from a lifted shell, a stretch of turf where peacocks could promenade. Something must be done with the brook, which was now only a brook, running through ferns. Already Christabel saw herself and the twins and the dogs photographed all over the place, saw the photographs reproduced in magazines and Sunday papers.

She had decided it was better that she and Nick should be simple-hearted children and picnic in the sunshine, for Mrs. Johansen never rose above chops and string beans when one telephoned. So they had thermos bottles of frosty cocktails, hot soup, hot coffee, yellow cream; and sandwiches with foie gras, thick, not just scraped on, besides the chicken in aspic, dark with truffles, the small cream cheeses, and wild-strawberry jam. "Here on the grass," Nick had decreed. "I don't like your quaint, delightful dining room."

"Polite!"

"Thank God we're not that any more. Doesn't it seem funny, now, that we hated each other so at first that every word was the essence of politeness?"

"Cold, cold politeness. But I never hated you. I simply considered you a young man so handsome that you would probably bore me to death."

"You turn my head."

She gave him a glance. "You wound me by your dislike of my beautiful dining room."

"*Yes*, I do! What a joke on the people who don't realize that you did it with your tongue in your cheek. As a delicate burlesque, it's perfect—every detail. The ears of corn hung from the ceiling, the infant pugilist in panta-lettes over the mantelpiece, ready to sock some one with a rose, and that supreme touch of satire, the shelves of colored glass across the windows, shutting out the view."

"You're a very penetrating person. Most people take that room perfectly seriously."

"And you let them, and laugh at them behind their backs. Christabel, you're a little devil!"

Christabel! He called me Christabel! First, Mrs. Carey. Then, for a long time, you. Now, at last, Christabel.

Nick! Nick!

And she suddenly flung out her arms, she cried, her voice enchanting in its sincerity: "I can hardly bear it! I can't bear it! I'm so happy!"

"Why —— ?"

She couldn't say, because you called me Christabel. And although the breeze, bringing a drift of fragrance, the tender grass, a quivering butterfly, had a lot to do with it when she came to think, those were not the things she and Nick talked about together in their clear-

292

eyed, ironic self-knowledge. The bitter amusement of life was their mutual preoccupation, not its sentimental prettiness. So she only smiled at him, lifting a cigarette with fingers that shook a little. His fingers touched hers as he lighted it.

"I envy you, Nick."

"Why?"

"Because you're in love in the spring."

"Like a beautiful ballad."

"Yes, like a beautiful ballad. You're a lucky man, and a wise one, to have seen how sweet Ellen is. She's such a shy little thing, like a little brown bird in a flutter, that most men would have hurried past without even hearing the brown bird's song."

"Naturally, I think Ellen is perfect."

"Oh, she is! Be very kind to your brown bird, Nick, be very patient. Men have such a way of trying to change the women they love, once they have won them. They expect one woman to be everything—beautiful, brilliant, magnetic, and at the same time faithful, and sweet, and unselfish. Most of us can't be *every*-thing, you know. Try to be understanding with little Ellen. Don't demand too much."

"She has a wonderful friend in you."

"Thank you, Nick. But who could help loving her, once they really know her? I envy you both. Love is—everything."

"Love's a grand state of affairs, but rather a general one. If we were Africans it would make us put on grass bustles and run bones through our noses; if we were roosters it would make us grow shinier tail feathers. After all, wonderful and beautiful and all that as it is, isn't it all rather a joke on us?"

Christabel's eyes were deep in his. Oh, my dear, I understand, she answered silently, and said aloud:

"Thank you for trying to console me, happy lover. But I know what all that, being translated, means."

He lit a cigarette, took a puff, and threw it away.

294

"Of course you do. All that, being translated, means, I adore my Ellen."

Christabel had asked Ellen to go to the Farm with Nick and herself, that day. She was careful to include Ellen when she and Nick did anything together. Even when they talked together she would break off to ask, smiling, "What does Ellen think?" And Ellen, lost in the sound of Nick's voice, the look of the sleek back of his head, that made the palm of her hand ache to stroke it, would feel herself blushing, would laugh and stammer, and have to admit that she didn't even know what they were talking about. It was funny, she thought, that Christabel's kindness in including her was the only thing that had ever made her feel separated from Nick.

She hadn't gone with them today, after all, because Talbot Emery Towne had sent word he was going to England unexpectedly, and, before he sailed, wanted to see as much of *Tear Stains on Taffeta* as Christabel had written.

So Ellen had stayed to copy the finished chapters, smelling the spring in the country as she wrote, feeling the squish of the grass by the Farm pond, where clumps of paper-white narcissus would be unwrapping in today's hot sunshine, almost seeing Nick and Christabel, almost hearing what they said to each other. At lunch, while her body sat with the children and Mademoiselle, while Alfred offered baked macaroni and stewed rhubarb, her spirit was with Nick and Christabel, picnicking under the deep blue velvet sky. Now she was with them, a shadow, unheard, unseen, as they drove home together through the cold spring dusk under the warm light robe. The band that had been about her chest all day tightened so that she could hardly breathe.

I'm crazy, she scolded herself. It's just because I'm tired. I'm not jealous. I'm *glad* they like each other. I hope they have a lovely day.

I *am* jealous ——

No, I'm not, I'm not!

296

She typed:

"A painted sky where rosy little loves rolled in clouds that cast no shadows on courtiers in mulberry and citron-yellow, pausing by a fountain's silver fronds, or on powdered ladies melancholy under green fountains of trees. Painted love, painted laughter, painted tears, covered the walls surrounding the vast central emptiness."

That ended what Christabel had done. Ellen arched her back to stop its aching, stretched out her arms and grasped handfuls of nothing.

She was starved for air. She would take the typescript the few blocks to Mr. Towne's. She pulled on her hat, not looking into the mirror. She knew she was a sight, but she was too tired even to powder her nose for anyone but Nick, who wouldn't see her.

But, coming down the shadowed stairs, she saw Nick and Christabel standing in a pool of light in the hall. Christabel was smiling, spring freshness about her like a radiance. Nick was almost frowning. They looked at each other silently, as motionless as if they held between them a brimming cup that must not be spilled.

Nothing told Ellen what to do. Feeling infinitely unwanted, infinitely alone, she stood there stupidly, not moving, until they lifted their faces to her, calling her down, telling her how they had missed her.

"Look! Nick picked all *my* narcissus for you!"

"Ellen, precious, you look tired to death!"

"I'll keep her in bed tomorrow morning, Nick."

She saw the white flowers with their vermilion-rimmed golden centers with crystal clearness, she heard Nick's voice and Christabel's as if she had never really heard before. Christabel's hand was through her arm, Nick's hand crushed her fingers. It is all right, she told herself, not believing. They love me and I love them. It's all right. Nick is here.

I'm all alone ——

No, no! Nick is here!

I'm alone.

298

Chapter Twenty-One

ELLEN, bringing Uncle Johnnie an armful of midsummer flowers with Christabel's love, told him her little news of the Farm. Christabel's roses had taken first prize at the Flower Show; Curtis was playing golf at the National over the week-end, for Christabel had decided he needed the change; Michael and Marigold had a new roan pony that they had named Black Beauty and Christabel had re-named Monsieur Patapon; Christabel's roses had taken first prize at the Flower Show ——

Had she told him that before? Her head was humming; she couldn't quite remember. She was so sleepy in the daytime now, so sleep-less at night. If I could only go to bed, she would think, starving for sleep, but when she was in bed the thoughts would begin, forcing her eyelids open, stretching her body tense.

"You shouldn't have come to town on such a hot day," Uncle Johnnie said.

"There were errands. I had to see a new kitchen-maid, and then I thought Nick was going to drive out with me—he's coming for the week-end. But he must have misunderstood. They said at the office he'd already gone out by train."

She had thought that perhaps everything would be as it used to be if they had that hour together. Perhaps she could really believe what she tried to believe, what Nick kept telling her, that she imagined things. But Nick was at the Farm already. He and Christabel would be having tea now, in shadow under the beech tree. Christabel cool in thin white. Christabel, who never exasperated Nick by being jealous and stiff and stupid ——

He'll be as disappointed as I am when he realizes that I was to bring him out, she tried to reassure herself. Will he be? cold doubt asked. She turned away from the feeling, never before put into words, that made her tremble. Nick doesn't want to be alone with me.

"Nick and Christabel are great friends now. I'm so happy about it," she forced herself to say, hearing Nick's voice speaking of Christabel, "Why Ellen, darling, I never knew you to be catty about anyone before."

"I remember how miserable you said it made you when they didn't like each other, and how hard you were working to bring them together. So you've been successful."

"Nick sees now how beautiful she is, and how brilliant," Ellen said, keeping her voice steady. But tears overflowed; she couldn't stop them. She tried to wipe them away, but they kept on.

"Don't mind me," Uncle Johnnie said. "Go ahead and get soaking wet. It's a comfort to you and a compliment to me, and we'll get you dry before my capable lion-tamer comes back in all her starch. Do you think your Nick is in love with Christabel?"

"Please excuse me—it's just because it's so hot and I haven't been sleeping. No, not yet. He's fascinated and excited, that's all so far.

But I'm frightened. He keeps telling me over and over how much he loves me—I think he's telling himself. He's wonderful to me this summer, as if he was sorry for me and trying to make up to me for something. And after he's been with Christabel he sort of laughs about her to me—but I'm frightened. She's working so hard to get him. It's all been so gradual, and yet now I feel as if it had all happened in a minute, and I ask myself what *has* happened, and I don't know. There isn't anything definite. Only first she bored him and he really disliked her, and then I kept telling him how lovely she was to me, and how generous, so for my sake he used to talk to her when he didn't want to. And she was so interested in everything that interested him. She got books and books on landscape gardening, she read for hours, she got to know more than he did about Alpine flowers for rock gardens, for instance. And she made him sorry for her. He told me how unhappily married she was, and yet how brave and loyal. I don't know

302

how she does it; she makes them feel as if they
had guessed it all themselves, without her telling them. And she let him do things for her
that made him feel kind and important. He
helped her with lots of *Tear Stains on Taffeta* ——"

Uncle Johnnie looked his question.

"That's her new book. He helped her with
all the parts about old French gardens. He
thinks she's wonderful now, and I understand.
I used to think so, too. Only now I'm terrified
because I think she's fascinating him more and
more. I'm terrified, and I'm sick with
jealousy."

She was silent for a moment, clasping and
unclasping her shaking hands. Then she burst
out:

"The thing I can't bear is that she's made
Nick look silly. I can't bear to see *Nick* taken
in. I thought he was too big a person for
flattery ——"

"No one's too big a person for flattery. Why
don't you flatter him harder than she does?"

303

"I won't try to hold him if he wants to go. I won't stoop to her tactics." You don't dare, for fear you might fail, said the cold doubt that lay in her heart.

"I'm ashamed of myself, talking this way about her. I don't know what's gotten into me. She has been wonderful to us both, and here I am talking like a jealous cat."

"Christabel has always been rather good at making other ladies sound like cats."

"She *has* done wonderful things for me. She's always doing wonderful things for people. You can't imagine all the presents she gives. And she always includes me when she's talking to Nick. Poor little Ellen, we mustn't let her feel left out—that's the way I think they feel about me, or the way Christabel does, anyway. She has a way of talking to me as if she would be brilliant if I were *just* worth it."

Uncle Johnnie produced a large fresh handkerchief from under his pillow, and Ellen mopped her eyes.

"When he does things for me, she says she's

304

so glad, that she had hoped he would. She acts as if everything he does is because she's asked him to, as a favor to her. She sends Nick to me—*she* sends Nick to *me!*"

"And you receive him sweetly, Patient Griselda?"

"I haven't any pride with him. I haven't any sense. I only love him ——"

"Of course you may get a lot of enjoyment out of seeing yourself as a martyr, burning in flames of love and pain. That's always a flattering self-portrait."

"Oh, don't, don't! Only I don't know what to do. Help me!"

"He'll never really love you until you hurt him."

"I couldn't ——"

"She does, if I know her."

"Yes, she does, she hurts him terribly. She will have been simply lovely to him, and then she'll get cold and disagreeable and hardly speak to him, and he'll worry over what he's done, and nearly kill himself trying to get her

305

back to being friendly. I've seen him look almost faint with relief when she smiles at him again and talks in a natural voice. I can't believe it's Nick, sometimes. He's always been the moody one—I don't mean moody, that sounds horrid, but he has the artistic temperament."

"So you've done the smoothing and cheering and lifting. Well, my child, a smug self-righteous glow will be all the reward you'll ever get for that. Be selfish, make everybody work and worry, and you'll be adored. I don't know any surer rule. Brace up, Ellen! Grab your young man back, if you want him. The Lord knows why you should, but if you do, grab, and grab hard. Don't be sweet and gentle, don't go on helping Christabel. She doesn't need any help. She doesn't want him the way you do. If she loses him she'll suffer, because wounded vanity hurts, but if you lose him——"

"If I lose him——" Ellen whispered.

"He has come into her life, and he must

306

kneel to her, or she must be able to ignore him, and evidently she's not able."

"I'm afraid she loves him. You don't know Nick. He's different. She must love him."

"Christabel only loves one person, and it's the love of a lifetime."

"Not Nick? Do you mean Curtis?" But even Ellen, who in her heart believed people must love each other if they were married, didn't believe he meant Curtis.

"Don't be silly, Ellen. Christabel loves Christabel."

"Oh! I never thought of that. But then— why does she bother with other people? Why is she trying to take Nick from me?"

"She is a sea-anemone. She takes the things that feed her; she ejects everything else. A sea-anemone looks like a delicate flower, pink or cream or lilac, with its tentacles moving as gently as petals in a breeze, but it can send out a shower of stinging tiny darts, and it can grasp what it wants."

Ellen turned her head, and Christabel's flowers, cool and smooth, brushed her hot wet cheek.

"Oh, I don't want to hate her!"

"Don't hate her. Be sorry for her. She's gotten to depend on adulation until she's frantic without it, and, like all drugs, the dose has to be increased and increased. Be sorry for her, but, if you want your young man, fight like the devil."

"I'll try." She laughed shakily, putting her forehead down on his thin old hand, exhausted and relieved by confession. Then she went to the mirror, to see eyes as red as if they had been boiled, a nose glowing like a mulberry under the powder she piled on it.

In the mirror she saw that Uncle Johnnie had closed his eyes. I've exhausted him, she thought, remorsefully. There was almost no one there—the bedclothes were nearly flat. The tired old face was as transparently white as if it had been carved from alabaster. She felt

308

weak with love and pity. But as his starched lion-tamer came in with what she announced as "Mr. Caine's five-o'clock nourishment," he gave Ellen a look that sent her away laughing through her lightened unhappiness.

Chapter Twenty-two

Nick and Christabel had spent a satisfactory afternoon under the beech tree, talking of deep things. Conversation had had to be simplified and lightened when Ellen came back from town. Through Friday evening, through Saturday and Sunday, she had sparkled with what seemed to Christabel an artificial gayety. Ellen had often returned from calls on Uncle Johnnie with ideas in her head, but they had never lasted for more than a day, before, and by Sunday afternoon Christabel felt that she must be spoken to, very lovingly and understandingly. So before supper she knocked on Ellen's door, carrying a cornucopia held in a glass hand, delicately cuffed in glass, which she had filled with sprays of heliotrope.

"I've brought you a nosegay for your dressing-table, Ellen darling. I know you've seen this intriguing thing, but doesn't it look even more perfect with flowers? No, *really*?

Haven't you seen it? Why, I thought, of course, you'd helped Nick pick it out. Wasn't it enchanting of him to bring it to me?"

She curled up on the window-seat.

"Go on dressing and I'll just perch here out of the way and chatter a little. Nick's monopolized you so I haven't had a word, and I wanted to ask you if you were quite well."

"I'm all right, thank you."

"You haven't felt feverish?"

"Not a bit."

"You're sure? Nick and I have been a little worried. Perhaps it's just the heat, or perhaps we love you so that we imagine things. I don't mean you haven't been gay and bright, you have, unusually so, but I seemed to feel such an effort behind it, I was afraid you were ill and trying to hide it from us. You know we both adore you so when you're just your own sweet natural self, that it worries us when you're different. Well, I'll tell him we've both been old fuss-budgets. Ellen, tell me to go! I have to change my dress for supper, and I'm so happy and comfy here I don't want to move."

She watched Ellen brushing her silky hair, stepping into white slippers, pulling an absurdly childish dress over her head. If she was going to affect simplicity to the extent she did, she ought to carry it all the way through. It didn't go with the *Tabac Blonde* she was tilting out of a full bottle, certainly new, on to her handkerchief (what a place to put perfume!) or the lipstick that she had never used before Friday evening.

I ought to speak to her, much as I hate to, since I'm almost in a mother's position to her, or at least an elder sister's. Shall I? It would be so much easier not to. Shall I?

She looked at the lovely room, the soft clear colors, the white and silver of the bathroom beyond, that Ellen had all to herself, unless there were guests. Where would she have been, except for me? She had no one else to go to. Who would have been so generous, so patient with her lack of training?

"Ellen, darling, *don't* use that dreadful lip-stick! Nick and I hate it so, on you!"

Quick red stained Ellen's face and throat. Christabel jumped up and kissed her lightly.

"Forgive me! You know how dreadfully impulsive I am—I blurt things out, and then I'm broken-hearted! But it's just because I love you that I can't bear to let you go on doing things like that."

But Ellen's mouth was scarlet when she came defiantly downstairs, and she wore the ear-rings that Curtis had mistakenly given her for Christmas. Through the first part of supper she laughed and talked exaggeratedly, she threw herself at Nick, flirting with him, teas-ing him, paying him outrageous compliments. Christabel could see how uncomfortable it was making him, through all his extravagant re-sponse, and for both their sakes, to stop the painful exhibition, she changed the subject from personalities to old mazes.

Late last night, after he had gone to bed, she had found the book he had been reading.

Now she was glad she had studied it until nearly dawn, for she was able to ask just the questions that drew him out, that made him glow. Mazes were his new passion, and he flung himself into discussion.

"But it's such a specialized subject. How do you know so much about it, Christabel?"

"It fascinates me; it always has. Maze! Just that symbolic word—all one's life translated into box or yew."

"Which one do you think we ought to copy for the lower garden here, Ellen?"

"I don't know, Nick."

"Didn't you go through that book I brought? You said you were going to."

"I haven't had time."

"We've kept her too busy with tennis and swimming and talk. But you have a treat in store for you, hasn't she, Nick? I picked it up last night, and I *could*n't put it down. The sun was rising when I finished it. Tell me, Nick, could you—but *you* could, I know—plan a simplified one for me like that old one at

Beeches St. Mary? You know, Ellen, dear —— Oh, I forgot, you haven't had time to look at the book yet. I shouldn't have had, really, but somehow one finds time for what one really wants to do, don't you think so, Nick? Ellen, you're lucky! Do you know how lucky you are? Suppose Nick's interests were in stocks and bonds and golf, like—like most husbands! But a creative thing like planning gardens! How different! How wonderful to be making the world a more beautiful place to live in!"

"I'll read that book tonight, Nick!"

"Oh, don't bother, Ellen. I think it would probably bore you, after all. I don't think the Beeches St. Mary maze, Christabel, but there's a wonderful old one very few people have heard of, at a place called Lesser Monkton ——"

"Oh *yes!* The one in holly!"

"My Lord! you *do* know about them! I thought something like that, in box, within sound of the waterfall."

Ellen's strange flame died down, she sat pale and silent, listening to them, and only messing with the delicious peach mousse, which Christabel was greatly enjoying. Afterward she went to bed early—with a headache, she said, and for her own sake Christabel hoped it was that, not sulkiness—leaving Nick and Christabel on the terrace.

"More coffee, Nick? You can reach the cigarettes. Oh, what a night!"

"What a night!" Nick echoed, pouring another glass of chartreuse. "You look silver in the moonlight."

Silver Christabel, she thought, hoping that he did, too. That was the sort of thing Nick always looked as if he were going to say, and never said. That was part of Nick's strange charm, that he not only never made pretty speeches like other men, but he dared to say rude things, beside which compliments seemed insipid. And at the thought of his smile as he said them, she grew suddenly weak. I hate him, she thought. How does he feel to-

316

ward me? I don't know, I don't know. Nick, love me!

She realized that she was trembling with tenseness; she had held her attitude of easy grace so long. It tired her to be with Nick, for she never ceased to be conscious of how she looked to him, so that often her hands, her shoulders, would ache from the graceful positions she kept them in. It tired her to be with him, it tortured her to be without him.

She rose, stretching white arms to the moon, and stepped into the garden. She could see what she hoped he was seeing—silver Christabel glimmering in the moonlight through the glimmer of white flowers, against the white plume of the fountain. Moon Maiden. She bent and kissed a clump of white phlox.

Nick joined her, and they strolled up and down together.

"So fresh, so fragrant! How it comforts me!"

"Do you need comfort, Christabel?"

She looked at him without speaking. The

317

air vibrated with the cries of insects. Nick, kiss me, kiss me, she called to him in silence.

The sound of the fountain grew faint as they walked, the servants' radio grew loud.

I wish you knew how much I long to *hold* you *in* my arms ——

Her hand brushed against his as if by accident. He caught it lightly, swung it, let it go.

When I saw you, I knew
   I had found my only love when I—met—you ——

He has led me to the edge of ecstasy, she thought.

This *time* is *my* time, will soon be good-*by* time
   Then in the *star*light—hold *me* tight ——
With one more little kiss say nightie night, good
   night, my dear,
   Good night, dear, good night, dear, nightie
   night ——

They turned. The sound of the radio was drowned in the loud cool splashing of the fountain.

Nick, kiss me, kiss me. Her delicate slippers

were soaked with dew, but who could think of such a thing at such a time?

"You haven't answered me. Do you need comfort, Christabel?"

"I think we understand each other pretty well without words, Nick."

"We do. Too damn well."

The light in Ellen's window went out. Christabel said to Nick:

"We must go in."

"Yes—we must go in."

"We really must, Nick."

He kissed her. At last! I am dying of bliss, she thought, breathless in his arms. I'm not disappointed. No, no! I'm not, I'm not!

He went on kissing her. The feeling of being crushed increased, her face was pressed uncomfortably against his shoulder now. She pushed away the thought of discomfort, and tried unsuccessfully to push away the thought that anyone might see them, in the bright moonlight.

"Nick—*please*——"

He let her go.

"Oh, Nick, how could you?"

"I must have gone mad for a minute. Can you ever forgive me?"

"Oh, my dear, it isn't a question of forgiveness. But it must never happen again—never again."

"Never again."

"We'll never speak of it, dear, and we'll never forget. Love only asks to love; it does not ask love in return, or joy."

He groaned assentingly.

"Curtis and Ellen must never know."

"My God! I should say not!"

"We must never, never hurt them."

"Never."

"We must go in now. Good-by, my dear."

"Good-by—good-by!"

The lighted sitting room was a room she had never seen before, like a scene on the stage, ready for the acting of a play. Apricot, lilac, and soft green of chintz, shaded lamps, heaped silk cushions, great splashes of foaming and

320

spraying flowers. For a cold moment she thought there was a bland, an almost smug look on Nick's face, but she knew, she knew, it was a trick of the light. Who can enjoy heart-break?

She was nervous about how she looked, for one isn't at one's best coming in from moon-light and dew, blinking in the light, especially after such an embrace.

"I'm cold, Nick," she said, and, as he knelt to light the fire, she came close to him, close against him, for reassurance from the mirror over the mantel. He lifted her floating sleeve to his lips. A thrill, a chill ran through her as she realized that, except for Ellen, Made-moiselle and the children, and the servants, they were alone in the house.

She touched his dark hair with a white hand she couldn't keep from shaking. She put her head back, her eyelids were closing, when a reflection in the mirror made them start wide open. Curtis was in the hall.

Something saves one, she thought, flooded

321

with relief and disappointment. Something stronger than oneself. And she dropped her bracelet and cried, "There, Nick! There it is, close to the fender," as Curtis came into the room.

"Curtis, darling! Where did you come from? Doesn't Nick look devoted? But, alas! he's only looking for my bracelet. I must have the clasp fixed. Dearest, how *glad* I am to see you—thank you, Nick—but why have you come home?"

"I—I've got awfully sad news for you, Christabel."

"What? Curtis, what?"

"Uncle Johnnie died this afternoon."

She sank to the seat in front of the fire, and covered her face with her hands. Nick was still kneeling on one side, Curtis dropped to his knees on the other, patting her arm.

"I shouldn't have told you so suddenly."

"Shall I get you some water?"

"No, no. I'll try to be brave in a minute."

"You are brave, Christabel darling. You're

322

wonderful," Curtis said in a hushed, solemn voice.

"You're wonderful," Nick agreed, a hollow echo.

"I can't seem to realize it. Uncle Johnnie—*dead*."

There was silence, except for the brisk snapping of the fire. Then she lifted her head.

"Forgive me. I'm all right now. But sometimes—I have felt as if he were the one person in the world who—understood me—and now I—I ——"

THE END

THE HOUSE OF HARPER

NEW YORK

Publishers of BOOKS and of
HARPER'S MAGAZINE

Established 1817